**"Whateve
them safe**

He put his hand on her shoulder and she closed her eyes, praying for guidance, praying that she wasn't about to make a terrible mistake that would end in hurt for everyone.

When she opened her eyes, they were directly on his. She took a deep breath. "I need a husband."

He laughed but sobered when he realized she wasn't joking. "Okay, you're serious. I'm just not sure I'm following you."

Tears stung her eyes. "I don't need just any husband. I need you. The judge we pulled for this case is all about biological family. And he prefers married couples over singles. If we get married...we would be both."

"Do you know how crazy this sounds?"

"I do. I know." She raked her fingers through her hair. "I'm not taking any chances with the safety of the girls. I can't, Cam. I promised Glory."

Award-winning author **Stephanie Dees** lives in small-town Alabama with her pastor husband and two youngest children. A Southern girl through and through, she loves sweet tea, SEC football, corn on the cob and air-conditioning. For further information, please visit her website at stephaniedees.com.

Books by Stephanie Dees

Love Inspired

Family Blessings

The Dad Next Door
A Baby for the Doctor
Their Secret Baby Bond
The Marriage Bargain

Visit the Author Profile page at Harlequin.com for more titles.

The Marriage Bargain

Stephanie Dees

HARLEQUIN® LOVE INSPIRED®

Recycling programs
for this product may
not exist in your area.

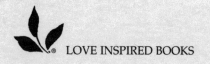

LOVE INSPIRED BOOKS

ISBN-13: 978-1-335-47900-6

The Marriage Bargain

www.Harlequin.com

Printed in U.S.A.

I will praise thee; for I am fearfully and
wonderfully made: marvellous are thy works;
and that my soul knoweth right well.
—*Psalms* 139:14

For lovely, grace-filled Gaynelle.
Thank you for welcoming me into your family
and loving me like your own.

Chapter One

Cameron Quinn looked around the tiny town of Red Hill Springs. Big pots of pansies, twinkle lights in the trees lining the street… Apparently the basketball team at the local high school was doing well this year—the storefronts were full of team spirit. It had charm, he guessed, if you were a person who liked that down-home kind of stuff.

He wasn't.

Cam shrugged into his sport coat, slid his sunglasses into the pocket and started across the street. If the Hilltop Café was still the center of gossip in this small town, he'd know soon enough where to find his mother. He nearly choked on the word. She'd lost the right to be called that a long time ago.

Bells jingled on the glass door as he pushed it open. Same brass bell, same clanking melody, the childhood memory surprising him with its intensity. Or maybe it was the aroma of fresh pancakes and coffee on the burner that had him instantly back in middle school, a broom in one hand, a doughnut clenched in the other.

He stepped up to the counter, nudged aside the

drape of tinsel someone forgot to take down after Christmas and took a stool. In seconds a glass of water was sweating in front of him and Ms. Bertie was greeting him with a smile. "What can I get started for you, hon?"

She had to be a grandma by now, but she hadn't changed a bit from the days he'd come in after school for a Coke before riding his bicycle home. On the best days, she'd asked him to sweep the sidewalk in front of the café and paid him in pastries. Her small kindness had meant something to a boy nobody wanted. He drew in a breath, the onslaught of memories harder than he'd expected.

"Just some information, if you have it. I'm looking for Vicky Porter. She lives here in town. Or at least she did."

Bertie Sheehan slapped the order pad down and rounded the counter to drag him off his stool by the elbow. "Cameron Quinn? Is that you?" She wrapped him in a hug before pushing him back to study his face. "Oh, my goodness, it's been so long. And it's so good to see you."

He grinned. "Thanks, Ms. Bertie. It's good to see you, too. I wasn't sure you'd remember me."

"I never forget the good ones." She nudged him gently back into place on the stool and climbed onto the one beside him. "Mickey, get me a burger and fries," she called into the pass-through. "I did *not* expect you to come walking through my door today."

"Me, neither, to be honest. But, Ms. Bertie, I'm really not hungry. I just need to find my... I need to find Vicky. It's important. Do you know where she lives?"

Bertie nodded slowly. "She manages a trailer park

about six miles out. Her place is the first one on the right as you go in. But, Cam—"

"Thanks, Ms. Bertie. I owe you one." He slid a twenty onto the counter.

She gripped his wrist. "Cameron, listen to me. Your mom's not doing so well since she broke up with Jerry. And your sister's death… Well, it hit all of us hard."

He didn't want to hear about how bad things were for his mom. He wasn't here for her. "I'm not—I don't—Ms. Bertie, where are Glory's girls?"

"Oh, so that's what finally brought you home." She rocked back on her stool with a knowing, somewhat relieved smile. "You don't have to worry. They're not with Vicky. They live with Jules."

The blank look on his face must've given him away because she laughed and pointed to an old photo on the wall of herself with her kids. "Jules—Juliet—my youngest. She and Glory were inseparable from the moment they met in nursery school. Those two were more like sisters than friends."

A vague memory surfaced of two little girls giggling in one of the back booths here at the Hilltop. "I need to see them."

"Jules lives at the old Parker place now, just past the Springs church."

"Thank you." The knot that had been building in his chest since he first heard about the car accident that killed his sister and her husband eased, just a little, knowing the girls were safe. He leaned forward and kissed Bertie on the cheek. "I mean it—thank you."

The cook came out of the kitchen door with a white container. "Figured you might need this to-go."

"Take it, Cameron," Bertie ordered, in her just-try-to-argue tone. "You look a little skinny."

Cam took the box. For years, he'd imagined that there was no one in the world who cared whether he lived or died, but he was wrong. Here was one.

The curvy road out of town was familiar and it was pretty, with pine trees sending long shadows over the pavement and bright yellow wildflowers crowding the shoulders. He noted it, like he did everything, but he didn't see it, not really.

Instead, he was in the front yard of the shabby little house where he and his baby sister, Glory, had lived with their mom and stepfather. She'd been six, a petite fireball of a kid missing her two front teeth.

That day, he'd tossed her into the air like he had since she was a toddler and she'd giggled before clinging to his neck. He still remembered how she smelled like cotton candy when she'd lisped into his ear, "Please don't go, Cam."

He was nine years older than Glory—the two of them had different fathers—and when their mother married again, he'd been fourteen. He'd stuck around for another year, until his new stepfather had kicked him out.

Glory at six years old was the carbon copy of their mom. Cam was a tall, muscular teenager who, with the exception of his green eyes, looked like his dad, dark skin and all. And it was his skin color, Cam figured, that his stepfather couldn't live with.

His mom had walked to the door with a defeated expression. He'd waited a horrible long minute—wanting her to stop him, waiting for her to say she didn't want him to go—before he'd gently set Glory on her feet and walked away without looking back.

He'd returned only once, when Glory graduated high school, but his stepfather threatened to kill him if he ever came near them again. He never did, but that didn't mean he forgot about his baby sister.

Now Glory was gone and Cam had done the one thing he'd sworn he'd never do—come back to the small town where he grew up. Because when Glory died, she'd left two little girls behind, and he was here for them. He might've been a powerless, penniless kid when he left Red Hill Springs, but he was far from that now.

He turned onto the dirt road that led to the Parker place. Cam wasn't sure what he expected, but the house that he remembered as a sagging pit was the bright white centerpiece to a pristine yard with a black minivan parked in the driveway.

When he got out of the car, the sun had disappeared behind the trees and a chill bloomed in the air. Decades-old camellia bushes with candy-colored blossoms flanked the stairs. A light clicked on in the house. He'd come so far to see them and now nerves jittered in his stomach.

He cleared his throat and knocked.

He waited. And waited, shoving his hands in his pockets and turning to look back at the highway, until the door slowly opened to reveal a pint-size version of his sister, wearing a pink nightgown and sucking her thumb. He lost his breath.

Her big green eyes studied him. "I'm Eleanor."

"Hi." Cam smiled at his niece, but inside he was reeling.

"Eleanor Prentiss, what did I tell you about opening the door without a grown-up?"

Cam looked up as a woman walked into view. Her blond hair was piled into a loose knot on top of her head and she carried a baby wrapped in a towel. Brilliant blue eyes locked on his and her feet stuttered to a stop, along with his heart.

He blinked, trying to gather the thoughts that scattered like leaves from winter-worn trees. "I'm Cameron Quinn. Glory was my sister."

Those blue eyes had gone ice-cold as she stepped between Eleanor and the open door. "I know who you are. What are you doing here?"

"Eleanor and Emma are my nieces." He could've told her about the promise he'd made himself, that he would find them. That, unlike him, they would never wonder if they were wanted or loved. But instead, he let those simple words hang in the air.

She stared at him for a long minute, then, with a deep breath, nudged the door open a little wider. "I guess you should come in."

"People have been coming to the door with food and presents for the girls for weeks. Eleanor likes it." Jules led her guest calmly into the family room, but inside, her stomach was quaking. Glory's brother had been missing since she was a kid. But there was no denying those eyes.

"Understandable." He glanced around the room. "Nice place. I remember it a little differently."

"Yeah? It's kind of a disaster right now. I'm usually at work all day so being home with kids is new." She grabbed a couple of toys and a fleece blanket off the seat of the club chair with the hand not trying to keep hold of a naked, wiggly, slippery baby. "Have a seat. I'm going to find some pajamas for Emma and be right back. Come with me, Eleanor."

"I'll keep an eye on her."

Jules hesitated. She might be new at this mom thing but she was pretty sure you weren't supposed to leave your kids with someone you didn't know. Even if that someone was drop-dead gorgeous and happened to be their long-lost uncle.

He held up his hands. "I'll sit right here in this chair. Besides, I wouldn't even make it out of the driveway before the cop sitting in the patrol car across the street pulled me over."

She paused midstep and looked back. "Ah, yeah. My mom doesn't hesitate to call in a favor. Sorry about that."

"She's the one who told me where to find you."

"Hedging her bets. Pretty much my mom in a nutshell." With Emma squirming vigorously now, and minutes if not seconds before the need for a diaper would become extremely obvious, Jules had to make a decision. "I'll be right back. It won't take but a minute."

The girls' room had, until six weeks ago, been her guest room. Now the walls were painted pink and the designer curtains she'd chosen so carefully had given way to sheers with pink and mint-green pom-poms. The dresser with its pretty flower arrangement and artfully placed picture frames instead held the changing table and baskets of diapers and wipes. She placed nine-month-old Emma on the changing table and tucked a diaper underneath her, mind racing.

Was he here to try to take them from her?

Jules had been there for both children's births, for Eleanor's first steps. For preschool plays and birthdays and holidays.

He might be their blood. She was their family.

She tucked Emma's pudgy little arms and legs into a sleeper covered in ballerina bears, and zipped it up. "Up we go, pumpkin."

As she walked into the family room, Cam looked up from where Eleanor had fallen asleep in his arms. Jules swallowed hard. His eyes were an exact match for his sister's.

She missed Glory so much. Every bath, every feeding, every time she tucked the girls in and turned out the lights, she wished she could turn to Glory and say, "Wow, what a day, but these are some amazing children you made."

Cam's soft voice pierced her thoughts. "I read one story and she was out like a light. I hope I didn't mess up her schedule."

"No. She didn't nap today, so she was probably ready. I'll tuck her in. Just need to get a bottle out for Emma." Jules put the baby in the portable crib with some toys and went into the fridge for a bottle. She ran some hot water into a cup and set the bottle in it, ignoring how weird it was to have a stranger in her house watching her do it, even this stranger with her best friend's eyes.

Jules leaned over Cam and picked Eleanor up from his arms. The sleepy toddler buried her head in Juliet's shoulder. "Be right back."

In the bedroom, she flipped off the light, leaving the room bathed in the soft pink glow from the ballerina night-light. She laid Eleanor in the bed and placed her silk lovey within arm's reach. Eleanor burrowed into the pillow and murmured, "Mama be here when I wake up?"

She brushed the wispy baby hair away from Eleanor's eyes. "No, baby, but Aunt Lili will be here."

"Mama with Jesus and God?" The three-year-old's eyes never left hers. She'd asked the same questions all day, every few minutes, right after the accident. Now it was only in unguarded moments, when it was almost like she'd forgotten. Jules wanted to scream at the injustice of it all, but instead she just smiled softly at Eleanor.

"Yes, my sweet girl. Mama's in heaven with Jesus, but I'll be here when you go to sleep and I'll be here when you wake up. Promise." She held her pinkie finger out to Eleanor, who gripped it with her own small finger. They'd been doing that since Eleanor was a just a toddler. *Pinkie promise, I'll see you in a couple of weeks. Pinkie promise, I'll bring you the best cupcake.*

For the past three years, a pinkie promise had been their solemn oath—a pledge given and received with the utmost confidence. Tears filled Jules's eyes and she blinked them back again. The pinkie promise had no power to make anything better for Eleanor. Not this time.

Jules rose slowly to her feet, grief a heavy weight on her shoulders, and another problem to shoulder was waiting for her in the living room.

Eleanor's eyes popped open in panic. "Aunt Lili, don't go."

"I'll be right outside. I'm not leaving."

Cam glanced up from the photo album he was

holding as she walked back into the living room. His eyes were glossy and her feet faltered. He gestured at the baby monitor. "I heard your conversation. Is it always like that?"

She continued to the kitchen to pick up the bottle and test the temperature on her wrist. "Yes. Not quite as bad as in the beginning, I guess."

Jules picked Emma up from the portable crib and laughed when the baby started kicking the moment she saw the bottle. She glanced at the clock to note the time and settled in the rocking chair with a sigh.

"It seems like they're doing really well." He closed the photo album and set it aside. "Eleanor's not that much younger than Glory was when I left home. Her hair's a little lighter, but she's got Glory's eyes and smile. Her spunk, too. It's…"

"Uncanny. I know. She's funny, too, or at least she was. Before." Jules paused. "People say kids are resilient. I hope that's true, for their sake."

He was quiet for a moment. "I don't know. I hope so."

"Cameron, why didn't you ever try to make contact? Clearly, you've been very successful as an adult." That was, if his fancy watch was any indication.

A frown wrinkled his brow. "From all accounts, Glory seemed to be happy. I guess I told myself she didn't need me stirring up the past. I thought I'd—I don't know—have more time."

"And now? Why did it take you so long to get here?"

"I was out of the country. Off the grid." He grimaced. "Way off the grid. I write adventure travel books and it took some time for my office to find me."

She hadn't expected that excuse. "What do you want? I'm sorry to blurt it out like that, but I'm a practical person. I don't like unanswered questions and I hate surprises."

A slow smile spread across his face and those crystal clear green eyes warmed. Her heart picked up speed.

Huh. That was a reaction to mull over later.

"I didn't know where the girls were. Or more important, if they were safe." He shrugged, spreading his hands. "It's really very simple. I came for them."

"And now that you know they're safe?" Her voice was soft because she was holding the baby, but what she felt inside had jagged edges.

He didn't look away. "I'm still here for them."

She shifted the sleeping Emma to her shoulder and patted the baby's back. "Do you know what Eleanor's middle name is?"

"No."

"It's Cameron. Her name is Eleanor Cameron." The words stuck in her throat—they were so painful and so hard because her friend wasn't here to say them herself. "I know Glory would want you to know your namesake. She'd want you to be a part of their lives, so I'm not going to stand in your way. But if you hurt them, there won't be a second chance."

"I'm not gonna…" He rubbed a hand over his close-shaved hair, impatience simmering in the move. "Okay, that's fair, I guess. I haven't exactly been present the past few years."

"Take some time to think about it, because the girls need people who will stick around."

He nodded slowly, rising to his feet. He picked up

his jacket from the back of the chair where he'd slung it when he arrived. "I haven't had a family in a really long time, Jules. I'm not about to mess this up. I'll see you tomorrow."

Juliet watched as he walked across the room, pulled open the door and strode through it. When the door closed behind him, she let her head drop back onto the cushion. Either she was doing the right thing letting Cameron into their lives—and she really, really hoped she was—or she was making the biggest mistake of her life.

Chapter Two

❦

Cam stepped out of the rental car and squinted up at the house he'd come to see. He'd called a real estate agent about looking at some properties. Jules had said last night that the girls needed someone who would stick around.

He'd spent his entire adult life traveling from one exotic locale to the next, moving on just when things started to get real. He was good at short-term relationships, sliding in and out of other cultures with ease.

It was the long-term ones that gave him pause. But that would have to change if he wanted a relationship with his nieces.

Tires crunched on the driveway behind him and he turned to see a patrol car cruising toward him. Perfect. Just what he wanted to do today: deal with a cop who wanted to bust his chops for no reason.

A muscular man with short-clipped hair and mirrored aviator glasses stepped out of car. "Cameron Quinn?"

"That's me." He walked closer to the huge cop, eyes on the hand closest to the service weapon still snapped in the guy's holster. Cam was a black man on some-one else's property and, like it or not, that made him a target. "Can I help you?"

The hand slowly extended and a smile spread across the cop's face. "You don't remember me, do you? Joe Sheehan. We were in the same class in the fourth grade."

Cam gripped Joe's hand, hyperawareness slipping away as he laughed. "Oh, yeah, it's been a while. I'm not sure you had those biceps in the fourth grade."

Joe chuckled. "No, I was pretty hungry in those days. I heard you were back in town. Planning to stay awhile?"

"Thinking about it. My nieces are here."

Joe nodded. "I know. They live with my sister."

"I forget just how small small towns are."

The cop laughed again. "Yeah, I moved back a cou-ple of years ago and it was definitely an adjustment. Fortunately, there are some advantages to everyone knowing everyone else, especially if you have teen-age kids. Ours can't do anything without their mom and me hearing about it."

"I guess that would be an advantage…if you're the parent."

Joe's rolling laugh bounced off the house behind them as a black sedan pulled into the driveway. The real estate agent, Cam assumed.

"So, you interested in this place?"

"I haven't looked at it yet." Cam glanced again at the house behind him. "I guess we'll see."

"Well, it's a beautiful place. Good luck…and welcome back to town, however long you decide to stay." Joe backed toward his patrol car. "If you're around on Saturday afternoon, some friends and I play a pickup game of soccer down at the park. And tell my sister I said to bring you to Sunday lunch at the farm."

"Thanks, I will."

The real estate agent walked up to Cameron and held out a hand. "You must be Mr. Quinn. Hey, Chief."

"Marjorie Ann, good to see you. I was just leaving. Nice to see you again, Cam."

The agent, an older lady with a short white bob, had a perky smile on her face. "Shall we?"

"Sure." Cam followed her through the front door. He'd asked for something near his nieces—which the agent had delivered—but this house was massive.

"The whole estate's in perfect condition and it comes with the furnishings. Everything's included, right down to the dishes in the cabinets. I know you said you have young nieces. There's even a beautiful nursery and a playroom." She walked toward a wide bank of windows and pulled open the curtains.

It was definitely way more house than he needed. When she'd emailed him the possibilities, he'd almost rejected the property without looking at it because of its size, but wow—that view made him glad he'd reconsidered.

Rolling pastures stretched out behind the house, swirling fog still lingering. A clear blue pond reflected the slightly rosy sky. In that second, he could see two little girls cartwheeling on the lawn. "It's very nice."

The agent's heels tapped across the wide pine plank floor. Her thick Southern drawl drifted back from the kitchen. "Gourmet eat-in kitchen. Top-of-the-line appliances. Fully stocked with anything you might need, except the food, of course."

He followed her into the expansive room. Once again his eyes were drawn to the windows and the large farm table in front of them. A family could sit and linger around that table. "And that building down the hill, that's the barn?"

"Yes. There's a small apartment on the second floor. Any questions so far?"

"Do you think it would it be possible for me to rent the place until the closing date if I make an acceptable offer?"

The older lady turned to him, a delighted expression on her face. "Why, yes. I think that could be arranged. I don't believe the owner has any interest in the property at this point."

"Write it up at full price. It's worth that, probably more." He could see the dollar signs like stars in her eyes and smothered a laugh. "Let's try and get this done today. I'll come by your office in an hour or so to sign the paperwork."

That brought an instantaneous furrowed brow. "That timeline'll be pushing it, but I'll do my best. Feel free to look around. I'll just head back to the office and get started."

He walked her out before turning back to the great room to look around. The space had warm wood tones and comfortable furniture. He envisioned a puzzle on the round table in the corner and a cozy fire burning in the fireplace. Laughter echoing off the vaulted ceiling.

Half-embarrassed, he shook off the thoughts. He couldn't shake off the longing as easily.

Cam tried out the word: *home*.

He'd been traveling for more years than he could count. A few months here and a few months there. He'd had all kinds of adventures all over the world and people paid him to write about them.

Was it possible that he could build a life here? Have family nearby? He wouldn't have considered it until he'd seen the faces of those little girls, seen their beautiful eyes full of sass and darkened with sorrow.

He wasn't a family man, but with that first glimpse of his nieces came a rush of love and a desire he'd squashed for years. He wanted roots. He wanted…

Home.

"So he just knocked on the door and introduced himself?" Juliet's older sister, Wynn, sat on a stool beside the frosting station in the kitchen of the bakery, her eleven-month-old baby sleeping in a stroller beside them. "Girl, that is gutsy."

Juliet looked up from the tray of doughnuts she was filling with pastry cream. "I know. I wanted to hate him, but I couldn't. It was obvious that he was blown away by the girls."

"Of course he was. We've all fallen in love with them."

Jules paused in her work to glance at her phone. Nothing.

"It must've been hard to come back here after what happened with his mom and stepdad. It was hard for me and I had you guys." Wynn paused. "Jules, what's going on with you? I've never seen you so tied to your phone. You've checked it at least six times since I've been sitting here."

"It's the girls' first day at day care. I'm a nervous wreck. It's only been a few weeks. What if I'm pushing them too hard?"

Wynn shrugged, but Jules noticed she glanced over at the stroller, where Addie Jane lay sleeping. "You have a business. You can't take off forever. Did they fuss, going in?"

"Not really. Eleanor saw a friend from church and she was excited to play. She's outgoing like her mom."

"See? It's going to be fine. What about Emma?"

"Stuck her bottom lip out, but didn't cry. The ladies in the baby room are sweet. They've already sent me one picture of her, playing with blocks on the floor." Jules slid a doughnut over to Wynn and twisted the pastry bag to keep the pressure on the tip as she continued.

"Thanks. I'm glad you're testing the waters before I have to put A.J. in there." Wynn glanced at the baby again. "She looks angelic when she's sleeping, doesn't she?"

Jules laughed. "Yeah. It's when she's awake that's the problem."

"No kidding." Wynn paused in the act of taking a bite, doughnut in midair. "How are you sleeping?"

Jules slid the tray of doughnuts into the waiting rack, pulled out a tray of vanilla cupcakes and picked up a different piping bag. "Sleep? I don't sleep. It's my first day back at work and already I feel like I'm failing them."

"I know this is going to be difficult to hear, Jules, but you're not perfect—and that's okay."

"I like being good at things." She paused in making her signature frosting swoops on the cupcakes as

Wynn snorted. "Stop it. I'm being serious. Besides, this is important. Glory left the children with me, but she didn't really give me any advice on how to deal with her mother, who's drunk texting me all the time, or…whatever."

"Whatever, like Glory's brother showing up?" Wynn licked her finger and grabbed a napkin from the table.

"Yeah, exactly."

"What does he look like?" Wynn tapped on her cell phone's keyboard.

"You know the biracial doctor on *Grey's Anatomy*? Like that, but with more intense eyes."

"Whoa." Wynn turned the phone around to show Jules the picture she'd pulled up from Cam's author website.

"Yep, that's him." Jules sighed. "So if the situation's not awkward enough, I'm also tongue-tied because he's that good-looking."

"That's so rough." Wynn's words were compassionate, but the laughter behind them gave her away.

Jules rolled her eyes. "Thanks for the sympathy."

"Anytime. So have you heard from Garrett about a court date for finalizing the guardianship?"

"No, but he said when he gets word from the clerk, he'll let me know as soon as possible."

The baby stirred and Wynn jumped up with a panicked look on her face. "Uh-oh. I better get back to the office. I know you're anxious to get all this finalized, but don't worry. Garrett knows this stuff inside and out."

"I know." Wynn's law partner was well-known for his skills in family court. But Jules wouldn't breathe a sigh of relief until the legal papers were signed by the judge.

She picked up the piping bag again. She had two more trays of cupcakes to frost and then she was going to check on her babies at preschool. Maybe that made her a helicopter mom, but she didn't really care. There wasn't anything she wouldn't do for those girls.

An hour later, Cam pushed open the door to Take the Cake, which he found on Main Street next door to the Hilltop Café. He hadn't been in Juliet's business before, but he was impressed. It had a charming homey feel, with some reclaimed architectural pieces on the walls and a couple of tables that looked like they came out of someone's barn. However, even those tables were glossy, and the glimmer of glass from the bakery case gave the whole place a polished, intentional look.

The door from the kitchen swung open and Juliet came into the customer area with Emma in some kind of contraption strapped to her chest. She stopped short when she saw him. A hesitant smile curved her lips, lighting her eyes. "Oh. Hi."

He smiled back. "Looks like you have company today."

Jules crossed her arms around the sleeping baby. "She... I went by to check on her and the day care workers said she was having a hard time going down for a nap, so I brought her back with me. I know it's probably not the right thing to do, but she just lost her mom and she's had so many changes—"

"Jules, you're not gonna get any judgment from me. I think it's fine."

"You do? Okay." She took a deep breath. "Sorry, still new at this mom thing. Can I get you something?"

"I didn't have breakfast. How about a cup of coffee and some kind of pastry?"

"Wintertime, I always have pumpkin bread. I serve it with homemade whipped cream. I also have apple Danish."

"Can I have whipped cream with apple Danish?"

"Now you're talking."

Today she was dressed all in black, which just made her blue eyes look more intense. Her hair was pulled back in a low bun. When she looked up with a smile, he said, "I bought a house."

"What? That's great! Congratulations!"

"Thanks. I've never bought a house before. I mostly live out of suitcases and overnight delivery boxes." He'd never really thought about how pathetic that sounded.

"With your job, I guess you haven't been in one place long enough to settle down before." She slid a piece of apple Danish from the bakery case onto a plate. A squirt of homemade whipped cream from a stainless steel dispenser and a sprinkle of cinnamon topped it off. It looked amazing. "One second."

Jules disappeared into the back and reappeared a few seconds later with a candle, which she stuck into the pastry and lit. "Now. A piece of Danish worthy of your celebration."

"Can you join me?"

She hesitated, glancing behind her at the kitchen, but picked up a bottle of water and eased into the chair across from him, her hand keeping the baby in place.

Cam blew out the candle with a smile and cut a

piece of Danish with his fork, but set it down again. "I didn't have anyone to tell about my new house…so I came here. Thanks for being happy for me."

She smiled, but her lip trembled. "You're welcome. I wish Glory was here to see this."

"Me, too." He took a bite of his Danish and groaned. "Jules, this is *good*."

"Thanks." She patted Emma's little back. "I'm just getting back to work, but luckily I have an awesome assistant who's been with me awhile. So, you just went out this morning and bought a house?"

"Technically, I made an offer and they accepted, but yeah."

"Where?"

"Now, that's the best part. It's next door."

Her eyes widened. "To what?"

Feeling really satisfied from the apple Danish he'd just inhaled, he grinned at her. "To you. And the girls."

"Oh. Wow." She paused. "The Grayton house?"

"I'm not sure I heard it called that. Supposedly some country star built a house down here and didn't realize it would be quite so quiet living in the 'middle of nowhere,' as the agent put it."

"That's it. Abbie Grayton built it. I think she was here for about two weeks before she went back to Nashville."

"It's a beautiful house with a pool and a pond. I think I got a little caught up in the idea of taking the girls fishing when they get older."

"You fish?"

He laughed. "I'm an adventure writer. Of course I know how to fish."

"When do you move in?"

"I already did. Or I will, I guess, when I take my suitcase in. I bought the place furnished, and arranged to rent for the month or so until closing."

"Wow," she said again, but she looked a little disconcerted.

"Jules, when I said I wanted to be a part of the girls' lives, I meant it. I've been on my own a long time. I waited too long to come back, and missed having a relationship with my sister. I don't want to make the same mistake with the girls."

He paused and looked out the window to the street lined with flower boxes of pansies. He'd been away a long time. If he didn't know homes like the one he grew up in existed in this small town, he wouldn't believe it.

Maybe it was time he reclaimed his past and brought it into the future, where he could make peace with what happened to him. "Look, I know I messed up with Glory—believe me, I get that. But please, give me a chance with her girls."

Jules put her hand on his and he felt a jolt of recognition. Kindness. He'd found it in every corner of the world in one way or another. It was more than he deserved.

She drew in a long breath and smiled. "Why don't I bring Emma and Eleanor by tonight to see the house? I know they'll love it."

Undeserved kindness.

He cleared his throat and nodded. "I'll be there."

Chapter Three

A few hours later, Jules's bakery assistant, April, stuck her head in the door. "Hey, Garrett Cole is here for you."

"Thanks. You can send him back here." She checked the supply of chocolate chips, last on her list, and stepped out of the walk-in pantry just in time to see Garrett push open the door. "I think my pulse rate jumped through the roof when I heard your name."

Garrett chuckled. "I get that a lot unfortunately."

"So what brings you by? I assume if it was good news, you would've just called."

He took a deep breath. "No easy way to say this, Jules. One of the family members filed for custody."

Her stomach plummeted. She wanted to scream and fought to keep her violent disappointment in check. "I was so afraid Cameron was going to do something like this."

"It's not entirely unex—" He narrowed his eyes. "Who's Cameron?"

"Glory's older brother. He showed up at my house

to see the girls a couple of days ago. But if he's not the one who filed for custody, then who?"

"Victoria Porter." Garrett pulled a sheaf of papers out of his leather case and handed them to her.

She reached for the papers with one hand and the edge of the counter with the other. "Glory's mother."

"Yeah. I'm so sorry. I know if the children's grand-mother had been a good plan for the children, Glory would've stipulated that in her will."

"She and her mom didn't get along. Vicky didn't kick Glory out, like she did Cam, but she is the most selfish person I've ever met. If she's filing for custody, there's a reason, and it doesn't have anything to do with what's best for the girls." Jules paused, tugged her bottom lip between her teeth. She didn't want to say this out loud, but she had to ask, "Does—does she have a chance?"

Garrett waved the stack of papers away when she tried to hand it back. "That's your copy. And the an-swer to your question is I don't know. We got assigned Judge Walker and he's known to prefer biological family for child placement."

"Even if the biological family isn't suitable? And Glory named me as guardian in the will?"

"Well, your definition of *suitable* and the judge's might be a little different. Once custody becomes an issue, the parents' wishes are considered, but aren't always followed. It doesn't make sense, but that's the way it is."

She stood and walked to the window that over-looked the street behind the bakery. "I can't believe this."

"You mentioned the children's uncle? If you can

get him to testify that the children would be better off with you, it might help."

"What if he sees this as an opportunity and decides to file for custody, too? I really could lose them." Her voice broke and she cleared her throat, desperately trying to hang onto her composure. These past few weeks had been the hardest of her life. She wasn't sure how much more she could take.

Garrett shook his head. "I don't know, Jules. I want to tell you everything's going to be okay, but this case just got a whole lot more complicated. Once custody proceedings start, it's really hard to know what the judge will do. This one prefers biological family. He also prefers married couples over singles trying to adopt. I've been in his courtroom a lot and he's very unpredictable."

She shoved her fingers into her hair, resting her palms over her eyes, willing herself not to break down in front of her lawyer. "This is horrible. Those girls have already been through so much."

Garrett put his hand on her shoulder. "We're going to do everything in our power to make sure they stay with you. In the meantime, make friends with Glory's brother."

Jules nodded. "We're visiting him tonight. Hopefully, he'll see us as a family—that the girls are meant to be with me."

"Good. I'll let you know if I hear anything else."

She watched through a blur of tears as Garrett walked back out through the door. The girls were her responsibility now. Glory and her brother had both suffered at the hands of a mom too interested in her own comfort to put them first. Jules would never let that happen to Eleanor and Emma—no matter what she had to do.

Cam placed the few items he'd picked up at the grocery store into his giant Sub-Zero refrigerator. He put a cartridge in his single-cup coffee brewer and looked out the window as the steaming hot liquid hissed into his mug.

It seemed impossible that he'd bought a house—not just because he was back here in his hometown, but because he was making plans to stay. But when he looked out those big windows at the stretch of green and the glimmer of water, it felt right. It felt like possibility.

The sun dipped behind the trees, sending long shadows across the pasture. He glanced at his watch. He'd expected Jules to be here by now, but she must've gotten held up.

He picked up his coffee and walked through the French doors onto the wide porch beyond the kitchen, fatigue settling in his shoulders. He didn't often second-guess decisions. His success and reputation depended on a certain amount of creative bravado. Making a decision to buy this huge house? That was out of the norm, but surprisingly, he didn't feel regret. He felt…hope.

When he'd seen his niece standing in the doorway of Juliet's house that first night, it all clicked. It seemed so simple. Yes, he was taking a big risk moving to Alabama, but so what? He'd built a writing career out of being a risk taker. And he'd turn the world inside out if he had to, for Emma and Eleanor.

He glanced at his watch again: 5:30 p.m. and no sign of Jules. Maybe she forgot? He didn't want the girls to go to bed without him at least hearing how their day went. He grabbed his keys off the counter.

A couple minutes later he was standing on her front porch, his hand raised to knock, when he saw water pouring out from under the closed door. Uh-oh.

He reached for the knob, pushed open the door and stepped into chaos. Water dripped from the ceiling, seeming to come from everywhere. Emma was screaming from the portable crib, her little face red and tear streaked.

Eleanor jumped up and down, making water splash, soaking her clothes and her hot-pink Mary Janes. "Hey, guess what? It's raining in the house!"

"I see that." He picked the damp baby up from the crib, putting her on his shoulder. Her little body curved into his, trembling and needy. He held her close, this tiny innocent sweetheart, patting her back as Jules came through the hall door with an armload of towels, her cell phone tucked next to her ear. Her hair hung in wet ropes around her shoulders, jeans rolled up to midcalf.

She came to a hard stop when she saw him. Cam froze, glancing up at the ceiling as a fat drop of cold water landed on his forehead. "So…what happened?"

She tossed towels on the hardwood floor in a haphazard pattern, words spilling out in a rush. "The water heater's in the attic and I guess it exploded. Water just started pouring out of the ceiling. The ceiling in the entire house is soaked and dripping."

He couldn't tell if she was crying or if it was just the water tracking down her cheeks. "Oh, boy. Okay, so why don't I get the girls out of here? I'll take them next door and get them dry and fed. When you get things settled, come over."

Cam could literally see the thoughts churning in her mind as she tried to figure a way out of letting him leave with the girls. He should probably be offended, but he did appreciate that she was so protective of his nieces—even when the one she was protecting them from was him. "I'll take good care of them, Jules, I promise."

"I know." She looked around her ruined home with a sigh, but her fingers were still clenched into a fist. "The water mitigation team should be here within the hour."

Cam wasn't sure anything could be done to save the wood flooring, and the ceiling was definitely a total loss. He wasn't an expert—by far—but it looked to him like it was going to take a while, maybe months, to fix this kind of damage. "Got it. Okay. Come over after you're done with the workers and we can talk some more."

"I will."

He turned to where Eleanor was tap-dancing in a puddle on the rug. "Come on, splash princess, we're going to my house."

Eleanor started toward him but looked back at Jules, green eyes darkening with fear.

Juliet dropped to her knees on the watery floor in front of the three-year-old, who'd known so much loss and change in the past few weeks. She gripped one little water-pruned hand. "It's okay, Eleanor. You go with Uncle Cam and I'll see you in just a little while."

Eleanor hugged Jules, arms cinching around her neck in a death grip before she let go.

Jules picked her up and followed Cam into the kitchen. She unhooked the diaper bag and Eleanor's backpack from their place by the back door. "You're going to need these. There's a change of clothes for each of them and Emma's due for a bottle at six."

As he grasped the bags, she held on a second too long. "Cam. Take care of them—I'm trusting you."

"Should I send my résumé over for you to check out?"

He was joking, but Jules tilted her head and smiled. "No, that's okay. My brother Joe is the police chief here and I already had him run a background check on you."

Cam was still laughing as he opened the front door of his new home. He'd worried, a little, about whether Juliet was the right person to raise his nieces, when he'd met her the other night. He wasn't worried about that now.

She had grit. And there was nothing more he admired than a little grit.

Juliet tiptoed out of the nursery in Cam's new house. It was ridiculous how perfect it was. Layers of white and pale gray and texture everywhere, from a faux fur throw on the floor to the bedside table made from a tree trunk. It was precious and both girls were sound asleep. She pulled the door almost closed and sagged against the wall next to it.

What a night. If any sense of reaching for perfection had remained before this debacle, and she would've guaranteed that it didn't, it was gone now.

The ceiling had literally come crashing down.

She shivered. She wasn't sure she'd ever be warm again after being soaked to the skin for so long, but when she walked into the great room, Cam had a roaring fire going in the fireplace and a plate of food on a tray waiting for her.

"I hope you're okay with pad thai. It's my go-to when I need a quick dinner." He glanced up with a smile and her stomach did a crazy loop-de-loop.

"It's hot and I'm hungry. Thank you." She sat on the edge of the hearth with her back to the fire and took a bite. "Cameron, this is so good. I guess you learned to make it in Thailand."

He laughed. "No, actually, Brooklyn. There's a little hole-in-the-wall restaurant that has the best Thai food this side of the ocean and a little Thai grandma who took a starving kid under her wing."

After inhaling an entire plate of food, she put the tray down and leaned back into the warmth of the fire. "I'm starting to feel like a human again. Thank you."

"My pleasure."

"This house is great." She wanted to be kind and act normal, but in her mind, she was reeling. The first blow had been the custody suit. One thing she'd had going for her was a stable home and business. Business was decent, but faltering without her daily presence.

And now her home was in a shambles for who knew how long. She had to do something to keep the girls safe and with her, even if it meant doing something drastic. And *drastic* was definitely the word for the germ of an idea starting to form in her mind.

"I like it even more than I thought I would," Cam

answered. "I spent all afternoon roaming through the house and the grounds and I still don't think I've seen it all."

"You decided to stay because of the girls?" Her voice quivered and she hated it, but she had to know where he was coming from. She remembered the beautiful, perfect nursery down the hall.

Was he doing all this so he could get custody, or did he have another motivation in mind?

"Yes. I'm not sure I would've ever come back to Red Hill Springs if they weren't here, but they are. And now, so am I." His face softened as he mentioned the girls, but still, she needed to know he would fight for them.

She tried to make the question light, but couldn't pull it off. "Have you seen your mother since you've been in town?"

The mention of his mom was like slamming into a wall of ice. He stopped smiling. "I wouldn't say I have a mother. So, no. Why would you ask me that?"

"She filed for custody of Emma and Eleanor. My lawyer brought me a copy of the paperwork this afternoon."

Cam shot to his feet and walked to the wide windows. She could see his reflection, muscles tensing as he fought for control. When he turned back, his face was calm. "Glory and Sam listed you as the guardian for the girls. She can't get them. Right?"

"Glory and Sam wanted the girls with me, yes, but the judge won't grant me guardianship as long as there's an open custody petition."

"Has she even seen them since the funeral?" He walked closer and his smooth grace reminded her of a caged tiger, pent-up energy and a hint of tightly leashed rage.

"No. She's been messed up for a long time. I'm not sure why she thinks she can raise two girls and I don't know why the judge would believe it, but I've asked around. The judge we pulled is unpredictable and he favors biological family."

"There's gotta be a reason. She doesn't want to raise them. She didn't want to be a mother to her own two children. There's gotta be a reason she's trying to get custody." He sat beside her on the hearth, close enough that she could feel the heat radiating from him.

"They have life insurance money from Glory and Sam. Quite a bit of money, actually, that hasn't been released yet. But when it is, it will go directly into a trust for the kids, for college."

His eyes narrowed on hers. "It will go into a trust automatically? Or that's your plan for the money?"

"Oh, I see your point. You think she wants custody so she can get the life insurance money? That's…" She floundered, searching for the right word. "There's not even a word for how despicable that is."

"Yeah, it is. Jules, what do you need? Do you need money for an attorney? Whatever it is, whatever it takes, we'll keep them safe, I promise." He put his hand on her shoulder and she closed her eyes, praying for guidance, praying that she wasn't about to make a terrible mistake that would end in hurt for everyone.

When she opened her eyes, they were direct on his. She took a deep breath. "I need a husband."

He laughed, but sobered when he realized she

wasn't joking. "Okay, you're serious. I'm just not sure I'm following you."

Tears stung her eyes. "I don't need just any husband. I need you. The judge we pulled for this case is all about biological family. And he prefers married couples over singles. If we got married...we would be both."

"Do you know how crazy this sounds?"

"I do. I know." She raked her fingers through her hair. "I'm not taking any chances with the safety of the girls. I can't, Cam. I promised Glory."

"I want to protect them, too, but getting married? My family, if you want to call it that, was not like yours. My dad split when I was a baby. My stepdad beat me and threw me out of the house when I was a teenager. I've bounced around the world for the past fifteen years. Trust me when I say I'm not husband material."

She leaned forward, her eyes laser focused on his, her voice soft. "I know better than anyone what your family was like. When your stepdad decided he liked being drunk better than having a job, guess where Glory ate her meals? And guess where she stayed when he figured out that she was more fun as a punching bag than your mom, because if he hit her, *both* of them would cry?"

Grief was etched on his face. "I didn't know any of that, Jules. It wasn't like that for her before they kicked me out."

"Glory thought you were the lucky one. Because you got away."

"I don't know what to say."

"I know." She took another deep breath and released it in a long pent-up stream. "None of that is your fault. But that is why I would do anything—absolutely anything—to protect them. You couldn't protect Glory, Cam. You were just a kid. But you can protect her babies. Help me protect them."

He grabbed her hand, gripping it in his. "I will. I promise."

"Then marry me." She looked down at their joined hands. "Please?"

Chapter Four

Cam sat in a chair on the stone deck behind his house, a cup of coffee in front of him. In his life of continuous travel, there'd been one constant that kept him grounded. Every morning, he read the Bible.

That sweet, tough little grandma who taught him how to make pad thai had also been the one to give him the Bible. In those days, he'd been an angry kid who'd known a lot of Christians in the small town where he grew up. It hadn't seemed to do him any good.

But Ya-ya was different. She gave him a job. A place to stay. She gave him a Bible and she taught him to read it.

He could never repay her kindness.

Cam tried to focus on the words, but thoughts of Juliet and her proposition from last night kept creeping in, destroying his peace. He'd tried to tell himself she wasn't serious, but what if she was?

What if her proposal was the best possible way to protect his nieces?

He'd never imagined getting married and settling

down. The thought of trusting someone that much seemed too dangerous somehow. He'd take zip-lining in the Andes mountains or BASE jumping in the Alps over that, any day.

But now that Jules brought it up, he couldn't stop thinking about it. He wouldn't have to trust her with his heart to get married to her, of course. But he'd have to trust her with *their* hearts, which might be even harder.

He thought of Jules, how she'd looked sitting by his fireplace last night, that warrior heart of hers on her sleeve. She'd go to battle for the girls. And they'd be safe with her.

Maybe it *was* his own heart he should be worried about.

The door to the deck opened behind him and what had been an undercurrent of anxiety spun into a low hum. His muscles tensed but he didn't move. Jules stopped beside him without sitting, and the silence stretched, her question from the night before hanging unspoken in the air between them.

He glanced up at her. From the shadows under her eyes, it seemed likely that she hadn't slept any better than he had. "The girls still in bed?"

She sank into a chair and set the baby monitor on the table between them. "Yes. I gave Emma a bottle around five and she conked out."

"You should try to get a few more minutes."

"I'm usually in the bakery by the time the sun comes up, so I'm not sure I could sleep in if I tried."

"You're not working today?"

"My assistant is opening up. After the debacle with the water heater last night, I wasn't sure what I'd be doing this morning." A smile ghosted across her face. "I never would've guessed that I'd be waiting for you to get back to me on a marriage proposal."

At the words, his chest tightened. No matter what happened, from here things would be different, for all of them. "Jules, I…"

She forced a laugh, her big blue eyes shiny. "You don't even have to finish that sentence. I understand. It's a crazy idea."

He let his gaze slide away from her to the pond in the distance, watching curls of fog waft lazily from the surface of the water. Canada geese were feeding on the tender grass around the edge. "How did geese end up in Alabama?"

"What?"

He shrugged. "I mean, did they stop here for a rest and the next morning one of them was, like, 'You guys go ahead, eh? I think I'm gonna stay'?"

She was looking at him like she was thinking about calling the guys in white coats, but tears weren't glistening in her eyes anymore. Instead, a hint of humor deepened a tiny dimple in the corner of her mouth.

"Geese mate for life, right?" Cam went on. "Maybe Gladys decided she was sick of flying back and forth every year, so Elmer just threw up his wings and said, 'I guess we live in Alabama now.'"

When she smiled, her whole face lit up. "I suppose you feel that Elmer is a kindred spirit?"

"Well, it is a little surreal that a little over a week ago, I was waking up in Marrakech, with no home, no family and no obligations."

Her voice was as soft and sweet as her smile, the slow drawl of her Southern accent taking him back to an earlier, nearly forgotten, time in his life. "It's okay, Cam. We'll figure something out about the girls."

Cam lived a nomadic life. As a rule, he didn't make long-term decisions. But Eleanor and Emma—and Jules—needed more than that. He reached for courage and hoped he'd find it. "I didn't sleep last night. I kept imagining what life would be like for Emma and Eleanor if they lived with…you know. If they had to leave you, leave here."

She swallowed hard, nodding but not speaking.

"They've been through so much already, losing Sam and Glory. And while I honestly think the girls would end up with you in the long run, what would that kind of separation cost them?"

Her face was a battlefield of emotion and he wanted to reassure her that he would make everything better. She thought getting married was a crazy idea. How crazy would she think he was if he told her that he'd been up all night not because he didn't want to get married, but because the idea of it seemed like such a tantalizing dream?

He turned to her and reached for her hand, but stopped short. Her hand wasn't his to hold. "Jules, there's a lot about this world I can't change. But in this case, I can change things for two little girls—two little girls who I already love. I'd never forgive myself if something happened to them and I didn't do everything I could to prevent it."

Jules pressed her fist to her lips, letting out a shaky breath. "You mean—are you sure?"

He scrubbed a hand over his short hair and walked to the rail before turning back to her. Regardless of what he said now, this was insane. They were both certifiable. "It's still a crazy idea. You know that, right?"

She laughed. "Oh, yeah."

"Okay, then. I'm in."

Jules launched herself across the deck and into his arms, half laughing as she threw her arms around him. Shocked, he went still.

She pushed back, her eyes wide. "I'm sorry. I didn't mean… Okay, I'm going to check on the girls now."

"No need to apologize." He managed an easy smile, but the turmoil spinning inside felt anything but easy. He took a deep breath. "So we'll meet at the courthouse after you drop the kids off at preschool?"

"Yes. Can we say ten thirty?"

"Of course."

Her face—with her wide, slightly dilated eyes—was a reflection of the range of feelings rushing through her, which should probably be comforting. He wasn't the only one going into this with a healthy dose of fear.

A cry sounded through the monitor and she snatched it from the table like a lifeline. "I've gotta run. I'll see you at ten thirty?"

"I'll be there." As she disappeared into the house, he turned back toward the pond, a knot in the pit of his stomach. But he was doing the right thing. *They* were doing the right thing.

Right?

Jules opened the door of her childhood home and was greeted by an enthusiastic silver German shepherd. She gave him a scratch, nudged him back with her knee and stepped into the kitchen.

Light streamed in through the window over the sink, giving the room a hazy golden glow. Fitting somehow, because as a child, she'd often ended up at the kitchen table eating a piece of cake or a muffin while she poured out the details of her day to her mom. It wasn't any wonder that she'd ended up associating baking with love and contentment.

She'd never felt more loved than when she was sitting at that kitchen table, soaking up her mom's caring attention. She could only hope that Eleanor and Emma would know as much love from her as she'd felt from her own mom.

After following the corridor to the guest room, she pushed open the closet doors and found what she was looking for tucked way in the back of the top shelf. She laid the garment box on the bed and gently removed the lid, barely breathing as she lifted her great-grandmother's lace veil from the layers of tissue.

When she was a little girl, she'd often imagined wearing this veil on her wedding day, placing it on her head as she did now and turning to admire it in the floor-to-ceiling mirror. She stared at her reflection. She'd certainly never imagined wearing it to the county courthouse for a wedding to someone she barely knew.

"Jules?" Her mom appeared in the door to the bedroom. "I saw your car outside. Are you okay?"

She faced her mother, warmth rushing into her cheeks. "I'm fine."

Bertie walked the few steps across the room and stopped to arrange the veil around her shoulders as Jules turned back to face the mirror. "Is there a reason you came by to try it on today?"

"I'm getting married." As soon as she said the words, she wanted to take them back. And that should tell her something about the absurdity of what she and Cam were planning to do.

"I see. Someone I know?" Bertie's expression never changed as she fiddled with the veil.

A giggle bubbled out as Jules turned to face her mom. "Only you would say that. Nothing has ever ruffled you. One of us kids could've cut off a limb and you'd say calmly, 'We're gonna need some ice on that.'"

"I think you're exaggerating a little." Bertie brushed an imaginary speck off Jules's shoulder.

"I'm marrying Cameron in less than an hour." Jules searched out her mom's eyes. By nature, she found excess emotion annoying and rarely useful, but she found herself on edge, in need of a little bit of Bertie's imperturbability.

"You know, my grandmother Elisabeth wore that veil when she married my grandfather. She had three very small children when she was widowed. She didn't have a lot of choice when she married my grandfather. But you do have a choice, honey."

Jules wished she could share that she didn't have a choice—not if she wanted to protect the girls—but that was the one thing she couldn't say. "I know. I'm doing the right thing, Mom. For me and for Emma and Eleanor."

Bertie brushed a loose curl away from Juliet's face. "I asked my grandmother one time if she ever regretted marrying so quickly. She said, 'The heart loves who it wants to love, Elberta. And I love your grandfather with all my heart.' About that time, he came in from the field, grabbed her by the hips with his dirty hands and kissed her, right in front of me."

"So she fell in love with him, anyway."

Bertie tipped her head and studied Jules's face. "Or she decided to love him, anyway. Regardless, I know you lead with that magnificent brain of yours and rarely do anything without thinking it through from a million different angles. I trust you. And back in the day Cam was a good boy who didn't deserve anything that happened to him. Hopefully, he's grown up to be a good man."

"He is, Mom. Everything's going to be fine. I promise."

Her mother kissed her on the forehead. "I know. Stay here just a minute."

Jules turned back to the mirror and stared at her reflection. Her dove-gray dress was understated, but was probably the most elegant thing she owned considering the majority of her wardrobe was imprinted with her Take the Cake logo.

She heard her mom reenter the room and saw her mom's sweet face behind her in the mirror. "You're so beautiful, sweetheart."

Jules's throat ached, and for a moment she longed to turn back the clock to when she was a little girl, when she and Glory would play house in the walk-in closet, when her mom would entice them to the kitchen with cookies and her dad would be coming in from work with a big grin on his face.

Life had seemed so simple then.

When she turned back around, a gold ring glimmered in Mom's palm—her dad's wedding ring. "For you. I know your dad would want you to have it."

The ring was a little dull, a little scratched and battered, but it was a pure sign of the love that her father had for her mother—and for their children. Jules missed him every single day. Her father had been a big man with a hearty laugh. The local chief of police, he could be stern when needed, but she'd never hesitated to crawl into his lap and lay her head on his broad shoulder.

He'd never met a problem he didn't face head-on. She liked to think she was like him in that way, practical and driven.

She lifted the ring from her mother's hand and slid it onto her thumb, her throat aching. "Thanks, Mom." A half laugh, half sob came bubbling up. "If I don't go, I'm going to be late for my own wedding."

"You've never been late for anything in your entire life. Go. I'll be praying."

Jules glanced in the mirror at her reflection one last time. Color flagged her cheeks, but the veil was perfect.

And she was as ready as she would ever be.

Cameron paced outside the small gray stone courthouse in the county seat a few miles down the road from Red Hill Springs. He glanced at his watch for the fourteenth time in as many minutes. This half-baked plan may have been Juliet's idea, but he should never have agreed to drive separately.

As he paced back the other direction, her black minivan pulled into a space across the street. The merry-go-round of what-ifs stopped short in his mind as he saw one long leg and then another swing out. He wasn't sure he'd ever seen her in anything but her work clothes. But today, she had on heels, a form-fitting dress and…a wedding veil.

His heart did a little stutter. He caught her eye as she crossed the street, a hesitant smile on her face. And had to steady his voice before he could speak. "Wow—you look incredible."

A trembling hand touched the veil. "I hope it's not too much. It was my great-grandmother's."

"It's perfect. I have something for you." He turned to the bench behind him and picked up a small hand-tied bouquet of pale pink roses. It had seemed like a good idea at the time, but he realized now that he didn't even know if she liked roses. And maybe he'd been making a huge assumption. "I, um, I didn't want you to get married without flowers."

She smiled down at the bouquet. "I love it, thank you."

He held out his arm for her. "Ready to go in?"

She nodded and slid her hand into place at his elbow as they walked into the building. Fifteen minutes later, license in hand, they were waiting to see the judge. Feeling like he did when he landed in New York City after months in the slower pace of a third-world country, he stopped outside the door to the courtroom, mind swirling with thoughts. "Are you sure you want to do this? We can find another way. We'll run away to Argentina or Uruguay or Iceland—I don't know. We'll figure out something."

"If you changed your mind, it's okay, Cam."

"No." He said it—and surprisingly, meant it—with a steadiness he hadn't been sure he felt, and the tightness in his chest loosened its grip. "If you're good, I'm good."

"I'm good." She said it quietly. And the doors to the courtroom opened.

The judge looked up as they entered the room and came down the stairs from the bench to meet them. *He* didn't look nervous at all, which seemed strange considering the dive-bombing bats in Cam's stomach. He could adapt to a lot of things, and had, but marriage was a new one.

The words to the marriage ceremony were familiar as the judge said them, but the five-minute ceremony went by in a blur. There were I-do's and I-will's, but the first thing Cam really heard was "You may kiss your bride."

Somehow, ridiculous as it seemed, he hadn't foreseen this moment, and he had the urge to ask her, *Is this okay?*

Then, with the weight of her father's ring on his finger, he cupped her cheek with his hand, slid his other hand around her waist and pulled her closer, letting his lips gently brush hers.

He'd made promises before—some of them he'd kept and some of them he hadn't—but he'd never felt a promise down to his toes like he did this one. He looked into Juliet's eyes and he knew in that second that he could never find another person who gave her heart as truly or loved as sacrificially as Jules did.

Letting go of her would be…crazy.

Chapter Five

Jules slammed the door to her car and swung her bag with her laptop over her shoulder. She pulled her coat tighter across her chest. A front was blowing through and the north wind felt like it could slice right through her.

As she hurried toward the bakery and past the law office where her sister worked, the door swung open and a hand grabbed her arm.

"Get in here. We need to talk." Wynn nearly pulled her off her feet as she dragged her into the office.

Wynn's partner, Garrett, lounged at his desk in the back, tossing paper balls at the trash can across the room. He looked up with an apologetic wince.

"What's going on, Wynn?" Jules had hoped to have a day or two to get used to the idea of being married to Cam, but apparently that wasn't going to happen. She should've expected it; in a town the size of Red Hill Springs, especially when every third person was a member of her family, secrets were hard to keep.

"Oh, no. That's *my* question. Mom told me something that is just…so crazy that I know she didn't make it up." Her sister glared at her, hands on her hips, looking all fashionable in her cashmere wrap. By comparison, Jules felt dumpy in her typical work outfit of black leggings and Converse sneakers. She pulled her coat tighter around her and adjusted the strap of the bag on her shoulder.

Wynn snatched her hand and pulled it close. "Oh. My. Lanta. It is true. You have on a wedding ring. Jules, what did you do?"

Jules snatched her hand from her sister's grasp and fingered the unfamiliar gold-and-diamond ring Cam had put on her finger yesterday. It was beautiful, catching the cold winter light in a million tiny sparkles.

And it felt like it weighed five hundred pounds on her finger. She slid her hand into her hair, rubbing the back of her neck. This was the conversation Jules had been dreading. Of everyone in the world, Wynn knew her the best. She even knew how scared Jules was of losing the girls. And despite the fact that Wynn had made some spectacular mistakes in her life, she always seemed to have it together.

"Well?"

Jules cleared her throat. "Garrett said—"

Alarm flashed across Garrett's face as his feet hit the floor. "Oh, no, don't even try that. Garrett said make friends with the uncle. Garrett said try to get the uncle on your side. Garrett did not tell you to pledge your undying love and the next fifty years of your life to the uncle."

Jules took a deep breath. "You're right—you're right. He didn't. But I did. Marry him, I mean. So you're both going to have to deal with it."

Wynn rubbed a hand across her eyes. "I can't believe you did this. You—the person who has to consult her calendar before she decides to brush her teeth in the morning—just up and got married. What were you thinking?"

Jules shook her head. It wasn't like it was a complicated decision. Could it really be that hard for Wynn to understand? "It's actually very simple. I may not have birthed Eleanor and Emma, but they're mine to protect. There's nothing I wouldn't do for them. Does that clear things up for you?"

Wynn rocked back on her heels. She glanced at the portable crib where her baby girl lay sleeping, and shook her head with a small shrug. "Okay. I get it—I do. I just hope you know what you're doing."

Jules met her sister's eyes, so much like hers that they could be identical. The truth slipped out before she could stop it. "I hope so, too."

"Do you really think the judge will buy it?" Wynn turned to Garrett. "Do *you*?"

He leaned forward, his earnest face and unruly brown hair a counterpoint to Wynn's polished beauty. "I don't know, but if it's going to have a chance, you're going to have to act like it's a genuine relationship."

"Agreed." Wynn nodded and turned back to Jules. "Family lunch on Sunday. We'll have a cake and take pictures, like a reception. You better make it look real."

"I will. *We* will." Jules looked at the two of them. "Can I go now? Apparently I have to plan a wedding cake for Sunday."

Wynn gripped her by the shoulders, tears suddenly springing into her eyes as she peered into Jules's.

"I need to know you're okay. You're my sister and I love you."

"I know. I love you, too."

She wasn't okay. She was really far from okay. She felt like she was chasing after her life as it spun away from her, like some kind of rogue tornado.

As the door swung closed behind her and she took a bracing breath of the cold air, her sister's words rang in her ear. *You better make it look real.*

Her marriage to Cam might be a marriage in name only, but it felt like the realest thing that ever happened to her.

Sunday afternoon at Red Hill Farm was no joke. Cam glanced around at the crowd of people milling about. It seemed like Jules's family had multiplied into a small horde. A horde with many, many children—some biological, some adopted, some foster.

"We'd better make this quick. The kids are getting restless." Juliet's eyes were clear and bright as she smiled up at him. She sliced into the cake she'd made at his house the night before—a two-tiered beauty with purple and yellow pansies topping the creamy layers of frosting. She looked happy, doing a good job pretending they were typical newlyweds, but already he knew her well enough to see the strain just around her eyes.

The pretense was taking a toll.

Meanwhile, he was aware of her every movement, as her sleeve brushed his arm, her hair sliding forward to hide her face. She broke off a bite of cake and offered it to him on her fingers, the ring he'd placed on her hand glimmering in the afternoon sun.

Even now the memory of sliding that ring on her finger seemed like something that happened in a dream, not real life, but here they were, having wedding cake with all her family, and then some, looking on. He swallowed the delicate bite and drew in a breath. If she could get through this, he could. He picked up a small piece of cake.

One of the older kids shouted, "Smash it in her face!"

Cam laughed. "I would, but I'm scared of her big brothers."

"As you should be." Joe crossed his arms and stared pointedly at Cam, a move that brought a cackle from the gallery of kids watching them, who apparently already suspected Joe was a softy under the big tough police chief exterior.

Cam held the cake out, meeting Juliet's eyes, raising an eyebrow in silent acknowledgment that this moment between them was so incredibly awkward. As gently as possible, he popped the piece of cake into her mouth, laughing as she tried to be graceful and ended up with frosting on her cheek.

"The bride and groom feeding each other symbolizes their commitment to care for one another in marriage." She looked up, blushed again. "I know all kinds of random facts. Hazards of making wedding cakes for a living."

"I didn't know that." He held her gaze as she rubbed a smudge of frosting from his bottom lip, a gesture that seemed intimate—more intimate even than the kiss they'd shared at the small ceremony.

"But we will. Take care of each other." He cleared

his throat and looked around. "This cake is incredible. Do we have to share it?"

"Yes," Juliet's sister-in-law Jordan interjected. "Don't even joke about not sharing cake."

Jules gave him a little shove. "No worries, Jordan. I know where to get more if we run out."

Jordan, sporting a growing baby bump and carrying a camera, grinned. "Glad that's settled. Cam, give her a kiss for the camera and you can be done and I can have a piece—I mean, the kids can have a piece."

Just a kiss and you can be done. As if it were really that easy. Cam smiled at Jules and slid his hand across the small of her back to draw her closer to him. She looked beautiful in a simple lace shirt and jeans, her hair loose around her shoulders. He grazed his fingertips down her cheek to her jawline, tipped her face toward him and leaned forward, his eyes lingering on hers.

She might be the toughest woman he'd ever met. She rarely showed vulnerability. Almost never showed fear. But in her eyes today, he saw a fragile hope, and that tiny hint of exposure sliced him to the core.

He brushed his lips across hers, and when someone— most likely one of the teenagers—shouted, "Oh, come on. That's not a real kiss," he swung her into a low dip and kissed her thoroughly, to the delight of the crowd of family surrounding them.

He'd expected the shock of awareness. What he hadn't bargained on was the jolt of recognition. The soul-deep knowledge that this woman was his wife.

Except that she wasn't. Not really.

He lifted her, laughing, to her feet.

Her face flushing pink, she picked up her plastic

champagne-style glass of sparkling cider from the table and lifted it to the crowd of family as she fanned herself with the other hand. "To marriage."

"Hear, hear!" Her brother Ash raised his glass and winked at his wife, Jordan.

"Heads up!" A skinny teenage boy rammed his way through the crowd of people around the table as a football hurtled toward the cake table.

Cam stuck out a hand and snagged the ball out of the air, saving the cake from disaster.

"Hey, cool, thanks. Great catch." The teenager stuck out his hand. "I'm Deke. Wanna play?"

Cam shrugged. "I'm the groom, man. Not sure if football is in the cards for me today."

Jules laughed. "Go play. I'm going to cut some cake for the kids. And Jordan."

"Thanks!" He kissed her on the cheek, an unconscious gesture that nonetheless had him faltering for a second before Deke pulled on his arm.

"Come on, Cam. If I stand still too long, Ms. Claire comes up with some kind of chore for me to do."

Cam chuckled and pumped his arm in the air a couple of times. "All right. Go long."

The kid whooped and started running. Cam cocked his arm back and threw a perfect pass. It hung in the air for what seemed like forever before it dropped right into his new buddy's hands.

He glanced back at Juliet's family—eating cake, chatting with each other, some still dressed in church clothes, most with children in their arms or playing nearby. He'd been on the outside of scenes like this one his whole life—wanting to belong, but never really fitting in. Truth was he had more in common with the foster kids who lived here than he did with Juliet's family.

Deke threw the ball back, smacking Cam square in the chest. His arms closed around it automatically. He smiled. "You've got a good arm, Deke. You just need to work on your consistency a little bit. You planning to try out for varsity next year?"

The kid shrugged. "I was thinking about it. Never been anywhere long enough to play on a team."

"I could help you some, if you want. It's been a long time since I played, but I still remember a few things."

Deke shrugged again, a nonchalant lift of one shoulder. "Sure, I mean, if I have time."

The boy probably hadn't had many people in his life he could count on to keep their promises. That was different now. "I'll stop by one afternoon this week and—if you have time—we'll throw a little."

Jules caught his eye across the yard. She had Emma in her arms and a smile on her face. She'd surprised him today, although he should expect that by now. He hadn't expected that kiss. It had been a shocking reminder that this wasn't a game they were playing. For better or worse, they were in this together, and there was a fragile, tenuous bond growing between them.

He didn't know whether to be grateful or scared out of his mind.

Jules looked up from wiping frosting off Emma's chin and caught Cam's eye. He smiled at her and, even across the yard, she could feel the connection between them. It was so odd that just a month ago she'd been independent. Single. Living her life, not even aware that huge change was coming.

What-ifs weren't helpful. Practical, pragmatic people didn't look back and wish they'd taken the time for that one long soak in the tub with a paperback romance.

But oh, she wished she had.

A bloodcurdling screech sounded across the yard, from near the playground area. From the looks of it, eight-year-old Ty had gotten in trouble and objected to Joe sitting him in time-out for a few minutes. He'd flung himself at Joe, fists flying. Joe held the little boy at arm's length while he flailed and hurled nasty words at his foster father.

Eleanor, who'd been happily playing in the playhouse with Jordan and Ash's little boy, began to cry, which then set Levi off, and before Jules could blink, half the kids were crying.

Cam was closer to the playhouse than she was, and seconds later, he scooped Eleanor into his arms and dipped his head toward hers to say something into her ear.

Joe's wife, Claire, along with a couple of the older girls, started rounding up the other kids. "Come on, guys. Family lunch is over. Time for chores, baths, homework. You know who you are and what you should be doing."

There were a few assorted grumbles and groans, but the tension that had seemed palpable when Ty started screaming seemed eased by Claire taking charge.

"You ready to head home? I think Eleanor's about had it." Cam appeared at Jules's side with Eleanor clinging to his neck.

"Emma, too. I need to stay and clean up, though. Claire and Joe have their hands full."

Bertie looked up from the lawn chair where she was holding Joe and Claire's sleeping toddler. "No way. You guys are the guests of honor today. I'll take care of the cleanup."

"If you're sure—"

"I'm sure. Go. Enjoy the rest of your day."

As they spoke, Ty's curses and screams settled into sobs and Joe drew the angry little boy in, lifting him into his arms. He eased into one of the many swings scattered around the property, with Ty in his lap.

"Is he going to be okay?" Jules knew many of the kids who lived here with Joe and Claire had been through some pretty awful things. She'd seen meltdowns before, but nothing quite as dramatic as the one Ty had just experienced.

"I think so," Bertie replied. "It'll take time but Joe's got him now."

The big, strong arms of Juliet's brother—who was himself a neglected kid and then adopted into their family—were the perfect place for Ty to heal.

"Come on, Jules, let's get these guys home," Cam said. Eleanor's head was nestled into his shoulder, her eyes dipping closed.

As Jules followed him to the car, she realized that just like Joe and Claire had responded as a family unit to the crisis unfolding with one of their kids, she and Cam were doing the same. They were leaving as a family, handling what they needed to handle as a unit. Maybe it wasn't a typical family and maybe underneath the surface they were anything but.

No…she wasn't going to think that way.

They had a ways to go to figure everything out, but, for the girls' sake, they were a family. She glanced at Cam, his face tender as he strapped Eleanor into her car seat, his strength reflected in the ripple of his biceps.

That kiss today had buckled her knees.

She almost wished he'd really meant it.

Chapter Six

Jules checked on Eleanor one more time, barely resisting the desire to tumble into the bed next to her and sink into oblivion until the next day. But that wouldn't solve her problem—namely one marriage of convenience to Cameron Quinn—only postpone it.

She padded into the living room on bare feet and stopped short. Cam was sound asleep on the couch. She glanced behind her as if someone might be standing there judging her, then took a single step forward where she could study his face. This time of day he had a shadow of a beard, but it made him only more handsome. She wanted to run her fingers down the angles and planes of his face, to trace the strong jawline.

Blowing out a breath, she gave herself a mental slap. That kiss today must've addled her brain. They were partners. Co-parents.

Maybe they were married, but they were *not* a couple.

She squeezed her eyes shut. *Come on, Jules. Get it together.* When she opened them again, she noticed a bakery box in the middle of the coffee table with a place setting on either side of it.

He really was thoughtful. The party today had been in their honor, but somehow they'd been too busy to eat. Now she was starving. She cleared her throat loudly and pretended not to see Cam jerk awake.

Cam sat up and pressed his fingers into his eyes. "Your, uh, mom dropped by with some leftovers when you were getting Eleanor ready for bed. Wow, I was out. Sorry."

"No worries. Today was exhausting. This whole week has been way over-the-top." She sat on the edge of the sofa and opened the box. "Hey, she brought a little bit of everything."

"There's cake in the fridge, too."

Jules piled her plate with berries, cheese cubes and tiny chicken salad sandwiches, and took a huge bite of one sandwich.

Cam picked up another sandwich from the box, skipping the plate. "I was hoping we could talk about how we're going to manage the girls this week."

Jules spoke over a mouthful of chicken salad. "If I go in before daylight, I can leave the shop around three and pick up the girls. But that doesn't solve how they get ready in the morning and get to day care."

He lifted a shoulder. "I can get them ready in the morning and take them. I think if you're picking them up and handling the afternoon, I can get my writing done during the day."

She frowned. "I don't want to not be here every morning when they wake up. Maybe I can rearrange my schedule to be home sometimes and we can switch off."

"I don't think that's a good idea."

She swung around to look at him. "What do you mean?"

"I mean, the girls need stability. They need to know what's going to happen every day and when it's going to happen. Otherwise they'll worry."

"I thought you were the winging-it type, traveling around the world on a whim, never the same place two weeks in a row."

Cam shifted back, away from her. "That's not exactly a fair characterization. I work with a plan, especially when things are important. And this is really important."

She shook her head. "I don't see what the big deal is if the schedule is changing, as long as someone's always there for the girls."

"Why do you think that kid had a raging fit today?"

Getting accustomed to his tendency to make abrupt changes in topic, she gave him a look. "I don't know... He didn't get his way and didn't like being punished?"

"Maybe a little of that, but at the heart of it is a hurting kid. He can't manage his feelings because of all the external stuff that's out of his control." Cam tossed the remainder of his sandwich onto his plate and brushed his hands together. "I'm not gonna have a meltdown when I don't get my way, but the truth is, I know what it's like not to have anyone you can trust."

His words stung. She'd done everything in her ability to make sure Eleanor and Emma knew they were safe and loved. "Are you saying that Eleanor and Emma feel like that?"

He reached for her hand, but she jerked it away and stood up. "Maybe we need to wait and have this discussion when we're not both tired. Give me your plate and I'll take it to the kitchen."

She grabbed his plate and walked away, hurt and anger burning in the back of her throat.

Cam took a deep breath. How did he explain this to her without her feeling like he was accusing her of something? Because he wasn't. He just knew what it was like to have a childhood where everything was on shaky ground.

He followed her into the kitchen, then leaned against the counter next to the sink, where she was washing the dishes. "Okay, listen. That kid today—Ty, right? He's lucky because now he has Joe and Claire and a slew of other kids who've worked through the same stuff before him. They're proof he can survive all that's happened to him. But it's gonna take time for him to trust it—trust *them*."

Jules swiped more slowly at a plate, even though he was sure it must be clean by now. "Claire says the kids sometimes try to sabotage a placement, even if having a family is what they really want."

"Exactly. It's kind of a self-protection mechanism. 'This thing I want so much is within my grasp but it'll never happen for me, so I'm going to blow it up myself.'" And wasn't that ironic? Because the longing to have a family was a wish Cam had buried so deep he didn't even want to admit it was there.

He'd been running from it his whole adult life. And he still didn't think he deserved it.

Jules turned off the water and dried her hands with a dish towel before folding it carefully and hanging it over the edge of the sink. "I noticed when Ty started screaming today, the first thing Claire did was direct all the other kids back to a normal routine. So what you're saying makes sense."

She paused. "Do you think Eleanor and Emma are going to go through that? That they're going to feel like they can't trust us?"

"I don't know. They're young, but the loss of their parents… I don't know, Jules. I'm flying blind here, too."

"But knowing what'll happen every day can help them feel safe with us, like they can trust us." She leaned against the counter in silence for a long minute. "If you think it's better for us to have the same schedule every day, I can work with that."

"You're sure?"

"I trust you. And if it's not working after a couple of weeks, we can renegotiate."

He laughed, but still he felt the weight of what they were doing in a way that hadn't sunk in before now. Today at the farm, realizing how much he was like the kids there, had been eye-opening. "I always wanted a family like yours, Jules. I can't imagine what it would be like to have a safety net like that."

"Now you have one."

Her words took him aback. Was it really that easy?

It didn't feel easy. True, now he had a wife and two kids. But that empty place where his family should've been was still empty.

The morning rush over, Jules cleaned the tabletops of doughnut sugar and croissant crumbs. Before long, there would be a solid stream of ladies coming through for one of her signature lunch plates—chicken salad and a fruit cup with a slice of lemon–poppy seed bread.

She'd missed the girls this morning, but Cam sent a selfie with them all dressed and ready for school. Eleanor's bow was a little wonky, but Cam and the girls looked happy and that was what mattered.

Cam had a perspective on the pain Emma and Eleanor were going through that she didn't have. And he was right. Both girls needed the stability of routine, at least for a while. They'd been through so many changes in the past couple months.

The soft chime on the door sounded as her mom stuck her head around the corner. "Hey, Jules. You got a minute?"

"For you, I've always got a minute. Want something to eat or drink?"

"I'm fine." Her mom paced the small bakery, perusing what was in the case, studying the photos on the wall.

"Mom, you're making me nervous. Sit down."

"Can you join me?"

"Of course." Jules grabbed bottles of water for herself and her mom from the cooler behind the counter and sat down at one of the café tables by the window. "What's going on?"

"Well, I guess you could say you've inspired me."

Jules laughed. "That's a shock. I can't imagine how."

"Getting married to Cam. You saw a way to get what you wanted and you didn't stop until you got it. Oh, Jules. You looked so happy yesterday."

"Um, I think you're exaggerating a little bit. Marriage

to Cam isn't exactly what I was after, which you know. So how did that inspire you?"

Bertie paused. Then she said in a rush, "I'm getting married."

"You're *what*? To who?"

"Mickey." Jules's mom folded her hands on the table, and on her left ring finger was a small diamond ring. The band that Juliet's father had given her was on her right hand.

Jules couldn't take her eyes off that ring. A tiny diamond winked in the plain silver band. "Mickey, your cook. Uncle Mickey. You're marrying Mickey." She shot to her feet, paced across the room, then back again. "Just to be clear, you're marrying Uncle Mickey."

When her mom nodded, Jules grabbed her water off the table and took a swig. Was this even actually happening?

Mom examined her ring with an indulgent look. "He's been after me for years now."

Jules choked on her water as her mother continued. And in that instant, images flashed through her mind, like cards shuffling into a bridge. Her mom smiling at Mickey through the pass-through, patting his shoulder, sharing a whispered conversation in the pantry. Had she really been missing this for *years*?

"I put him off until you kids were settled. Well, you're settled now and we're eloping."

Jules couldn't imagine being less settled than she was at this moment, but from the outside, she guessed that—maybe—it seemed like her life was now settled.

Wait. Eloping? "When?"

"We're leaving tonight. Mickey's daughter's having a C-section in Nashville tomorrow and he wants to see the baby before we go to Hawaii for a few weeks...or months."

Jules blinked. Tonight.

So *now* meant...*now*. "Wow, Mom. I'm— congratulations?"

"Thank you, Jules. But I actually came by for something else." Bertie reached into her purse and pulled out a thick envelope. "I'm leaving the café in your hands. In fact, I'm leaving you the café, period. Everything is here—the deed, the ownership papers, everything you'll need to be the owner and proprietor. I know the timing could be better, honey, but it was going to go to you someday, anyway. And I'm hoping that will help make up for it."

"Mom... I don't know if I can do this."

"You've done such a beautiful job with the bakery. I know you're the best one to take over the café. You can do this, Jules."

No. She really couldn't.

Seriously, *no*.

She'd just been left two children she barely knew what to do with. She couldn't possibly—and even if she did— "You're marrying the cook, Mom. How am I gonna run a café without a cook?"

"You'll have Albert until you can hire a new cook." She put a hand up. "Now, I know Albert can be a little unreliable, but he's been doing really well the past few weeks."

Albert was Mickey's assistant and he was a decent cook when he wasn't coming off a bender, but she couldn't run the café depending solely on Albert.

She couldn't say no, either. How could she?

Her mother thought the café was a huge gift.

On top of that, Mom had no idea how hard things had

been for Jules the past couple months, because naturally Jules wouldn't dare let anyone see her struggle. They might find out she was human. She shook her head.

It was too late to share that with her mother now. Mom was sitting here, telling Jules she'd been waiting years for a second chance at love because she wanted her kids to be settled first.

Who was Jules to stand in the way of her finding love? "I'm sure it'll be fine, Mom."

"Jules, thank you!" Her mom's eyes shone with happiness, and Jules knew she couldn't go back on her word now.

Her stomach knotted. She had so much responsibility as it was. How could she possibly make this work? She forced a smile. "I hope you'll be really happy, Mom."

Bertie bounded to her feet and snatched up her bag. "I can't wait to tell Mickey we're on!"

Jules stared blankly at the door as it swung slowly shut. She was a perfectionist. A doer. A handler. She knew it. Everyone knew it.

In high school, if the teacher assigned a group project, everyone wanted to be in her group. Give her a job and she'd handle it. She always did. But as she felt the pressure building inside her like a pressure cooker ready to explode, she realized she did have a breaking point.

And she'd quite possibly just reached it.

Leaving the small kennel by the door, Cam whispered to the puppy, "Shh. Don't forget you're a surprise. No whining."

He followed the sound of giggles to the kitchen

and found Eleanor and Jules at the table. Eleanor had a smear of purple frosting from one ear to her nose. Emma sat nearby in her high chair, happily kicking her feet and eating Cheerios.

"Well, what do we have here, ladies?"

"Uncle Cam!" Eleanor launched herself toward him. He snagged her in midair, making her squeal when he spun her around.

As he slowed down and plunked her back in her seat, she pointed to a mound of frosting and sprinkles on her plate. "I'm making you a cookie."

"Is there a cookie under there?" He cut his eyes to Jules.

She smiled, but it didn't quite reach her eyes. "Maybe? Everyone knows the frosting is the best part, anyway. Right, Eleanor?"

"Wight." His niece stuck a sticky finger in the bowl of sprinkles.

Cam held his hands out to the baby, gratified when she held her arms up for him to pick her up. He gave her a smooch on her soft round cheeks. In return, she grabbed his nose and chortled. He laughed and nuzzled her again. "I brought you guys a surprise. Hang on just a second."

He handed Emma to Jules, ran back to the front door, where he'd left the small kennel, and brought it into the kitchen. He had no idea why, but when he'd passed the sign on the side of the highway about Lab puppies for sale, he'd turned around immediately, compelled to stop. He opened the door and a pudgy black puppy tumbled out onto the travertine floor.

Jules gasped. And it was right then that he realized he probably should've talked to her before he showed up with a dog. Before he could say anything, Eleanor squealed and threw herself onto the floor. "A puppy, a puppy, a puppy!"

He sent Jules a sheepish grin and dropped to the floor beside Eleanor, laughing when the puppy tried to climb into his lap and rolled back down. "Her name is Pippi. She's a black Lab and she's ten weeks old."

Pippi licked Eleanor's face until it was completely clean of frosting and the little girl was laughing so hard she couldn't catch her breath. And that reaction alone was totally worth buying a puppy that he knew good and well was going to be a pain in the neck.

"Maybe we should take her outside." Jules opened the back door. "Come on, Pippi. Outside."

A few minutes later, Eleanor and her new puppy were tumbling in the wide stretch of grass in the backyard. Cam carried Emma, Jules walking slowly beside him. "I can't believe you just bought a puppy. Who does that?"

He'd always been an act-first-apologize-later kind of guy, but he'd never been married before. He scratched his head. "About that, I really should've talked to you about it first. Probably broke at least a handful of marriage rules."

She heaved a tired sigh. "I'd say so."

"You might have to make a list of those. I've been a little undisciplined for the past, um, fifteen years."

"I'd say you have pretty good instincts. Look how happy Eleanor is. Besides, he who buys the dog has to potty train the dog, so I guess it all works out."

"Eleanor was happy making cookies with you when I came in."

Jules glanced over at him. "Yeah, something you

said last night made me realize that when Eleanor lost her mom and dad, she lost everything. Even her favorite aunt."

"I'm confused."

She shrugged. "I've always been the fun aunt to Eleanor. I came into town with cupcakes and pinkie promises and presents. But when I became the mom figure, she lost me, too. I figured she needed a little reminder of how it used to be."

"And you needed a reminder, too?"

She looked at him in surprise. "Very perceptive. Yeah, it was a monster of a day."

"What happened?"

"It started out with my mom telling me she's eloping with her cook."

He snorted a laugh and then caught sight of her face. "Oh, you're really not joking."

"No. She left the keys to the café—and the deed—in my care." She stopped walking and he turned back to face her. She had her face buried in her hands.

"Is there anything I can do? Jules?"

She bent over at the waist, words gasping out with giggles, which seemed to him to be awfully close to sobs. "I can't even—my *mom* is eloping. With Uncle Mickey."

Cam had a feeling Jules had pretty much reached the end of her ability to cope with change. She'd admitted when they first met that she hated surprises, and her life had been one surprise after another for the past six weeks.

As she came up gasping for air, he said, "Sorry about the puppy. Probably wasn't the best day to surprise you with a dog."

She waved him off. "I really don't care about the dog. She's adorable and Eleanor needs her. There's just so much going on. So much to do, and I don't have any idea how I'm going to handle it."

"If I can help you with the other stuff, I will." He had a book to write, but he kept getting distracted. He'd never really had that problem before, but then he'd never had this kind of responsibility before. "I mean it, Jules. Marriage rules."

She shot him a genuine smile. "Which one?"

"The one that says you're not in this alone."

"Oh, Cam." She stepped closer to him, and because she seemed to need it, he put his arm around her shoulders as they resumed their walk.

Emma lunged for Jules, who obliged with a shaky laugh and settled the baby on her hip. She glanced up at Cam. "It's a lot to handle, but it's going to be fine. Truly."

Chapter Seven

I t wasn't fine.

It was so far from fine that fine was not even in sight. Jules was a planner, but plans had gone out the window along with her sanity about two hours into this gig. She'd been going from one crisis to another in the restaurant and bakery all week, until she wanted to pull her hair out.

And that schedule she and Cam had so thoughtfully crafted? Obliterated the first day. She hadn't seen the girls in four days. She looked at her watch. Well, make that five days. They'd be in bed before she got home and Cam had had them on his own, all day, again.

She'd say she didn't know how her mom did it all while she and her brothers and sister were growing up, but she did know. Her mom had Uncle Mickey.

There was a knock on the frame of her open office door. The part-time—now full-time—cook stood in the doorway. Albert didn't meet her eyes. "Lanna told me you wanted to see me?"

"You were supposed to be here four hours ago, Albert."

His gaze was glued to the floor. "I know. I lost track of time. I'm sorry."

Lost track of time, had a doctor's appointment, couldn't find his keys, his tire was flat... The excuses were endless and she'd given him "one last chance" three times. "You've either completely missed your shift or been late every single day this week. Albert, you know you're the cook now. This place doesn't run without you."

"That's a lot of pressure, Jules."

Yeah, no kidding. "Tomorrow's Sunday and we're closed. You'll have one day to think about this. If you want a job, be here Monday morning at 5:00 a.m. If you don't...just don't come."

His eyes bugged out, meeting hers for the first time. They were red and bloodshot. He was using and she'd known it. She even knew why. There were no secrets in a small town. Her heart broke for the kid who'd lost his girlfriend in a tragic accident two years ago. Her mom had a track record of bringing in the lost and the lonely and giving them small jobs to help them get back on their feet.

Albert could do small jobs. What he couldn't manage was being the full-time cook. And she really, really needed a full-time cook.

She took a deep breath and put her frustrations aside, because even though he was a pain, he was also *in pain*. "Albert, I want you to stay and be a part of our team, but I have two small children and a bakery to run. I don't have time to pick up your slack. You either have to get it together or you have to go."

He nodded, his Adam's apple bobbing as he

swallowed hard. "I want to help you, Jules, but it's too much. I...I have to quit."

Albert handed her his apron and ran out of the back room, nearly mowing down Lanna, her best, most consistent server, in the process. Jules rubbed her aching forehead with her fingers. So now what did she do?

Was a cook who showed up only 30 percent of the time better than no cook at all?

Lanna stopped in the open doorway. "He quit?"

Jules slowly nodded. "I'm not sure what I expected. I guess I'd just hoped for a different outcome."

"I can't say I'm surprised, but I'm sorry."

"Me, too." Jules scrubbed her hands over her face, got a whiff of her shirt and grimaced. She smelled like the fryer. All she wanted to do was get home and soak in a hot tub, but she had to stay and close up.

"There's only one couple out there now having pie and coffee. They'll probably be the last ones for the night. Why don't you go home and let me finish things up here?"

It was like Lanna had heard her thoughts, but... "There's still another hour on the clock, Lanna. I can't leave you."

"Oh, please. I've been working here for twenty years. There's nothing on the menu I don't know how to make."

Jules gave her a speculative look.

"Oh, no, you don't." Lanna laughed. "I'm not a cook. I said I knew how to make everything on the menu, not that I wanted to. But you go home. See your babies. This will all be here Monday morning."

"If you're sure." Jules picked up her purse and keys from the desk. "Really sure?"

"I am." Lanna hugged her as they met in the doorway. "You've always been so frighteningly efficient, Jules, even as a kid. Your mom couldn't have known how hard things would get."

"Things were already hard between the bakery and becoming an instant mother to an infant and a toddler." Jules shook her head. "But I have tomorrow to figure out how to manage it all. If you hear of someone who wants to be the cook, let me know."

"Will do. Now, go."

Jules barely remembered getting in the car and driving home. She was so tired her bones ached, but somehow she had to come up with a plan for the bakery and the restaurant, when all she wanted to do was get in bed and sleep for days.

She stepped into the kitchen expecting everyone to be asleep, or maybe to find Cam working on his laptop like he had been the past few nights. And he was sitting at the kitchen table with his laptop open, but his foot was on the rock-n-play sleeper, keeping a steady rocking motion going. The dog was sprawled on top of his other foot.

He looked up and, as tired as she was, she couldn't help but notice she wasn't the only one. He had a huge mug of coffee by his computer and circles under his eyes. There were dishes on every surface of the huge kitchen. One side of the sink was full of dirty bottles.

"Rough night?"

Cam leaned back in his chair. "You could say that. Emma's been fighting sleep like a champ all day. I think maybe she's teething? To be honest, I have no idea, but that's what the internet said."

She sank into the chair next to him. "I'm sorry things have been so crazy. I'm not keeping up my end of the bargain."

"No. I mean...I get that you're buried, but I'm taking care of the kids all day and trying to write at night after everyone's asleep. I'm running on something like eight hours of sleep for the whole week."

"I'm so sorry." She sat back and let her arms drop to her sides. "I just fired the person I would loosely call my cook. Or he quit. I honestly can't remember."

He didn't even react. His face was set in hard, tired grooves. "So...what happens now?"

She'd walked in here wanting only sleep. But the man across from her, incredibly, needed it even more than she did. Jules took a deep breath and dug deep down, trying to scrape up a reservoir of energy from...somewhere. "Right now, I take over for you with Emma. You get a good night's sleep. Tomorrow's Sunday and the café and the bakery are both closed. I'll take the girls all day and you can write."

"And on Monday?"

"I'll figure something out before then."

"I really hope so, Jules." He glanced down at Emma, who'd apparently finally fallen asleep, then he picked up his laptop and walked away. His broad shoulders were slumped in exhaustion—shoulders that had been carrying his share of the workload and then some.

He didn't say good-night and Jules didn't blame him. She wanted her life back, too. The life where there was a plan and everyone followed the plan. There was order.

Predictability. Yeah. Predictability was good.

She walked to the sink and turned on the hot water to wash out the bottles. There was nothing good in all this chaos for her or for Cam, and it was unfair to the girls, who needed them both.

Sleep won over writing, and when Cam stumbled into the kitchen on Sunday morning, he felt decidedly better than he had the night before. He poured himself a cup of coffee from the pot on the counter and picked up the note Jules left for him by the pot. "Gone to church and family lunch. Welcome to join in."

Oh, no. Not only had he slept right through church, he was missing family lunch, as well. He made record time changing clothes and jumping in his rental car to see if he could make it to the farm in time to stay out of the doghouse. Although, considering his behavior with Jules last night, he was probably already deservedly there.

Cars still lined the driveway, so maybe he wasn't too late. He slammed the gearshift into Park and jumped out of the car, his loafers skidding to a halt halfway to the backyard when he realized his shirt was untucked. He straightened and tucked his shirt in, then took a deep breath and blew it out. *Okay.*

He strode around the corner of the house and almost slammed into Latham, who was walking toward his car, carrying a baby, a mini cooler and a diaper bag that Cam was pretty sure he could've backpacked through Europe with. "Ah, hey… Latham, right?"

"Yeah." Wynn's husband bobbed up and down with

the baby, whose face was slowly turning purplish red. "Listen, I've got to get her in the car before she completely loses it. She's refusing to nap and A.J. without a nap is not anything anyone needs to experience if they don't have to."

"Sure. Know where Jules is?"

"I think they're having a sibling powwow in the kitchen. I'll see you around. Maybe we can get the little ones together sometime."

"Yeah, sure. Sounds good. Hope you guys get a nap."

"Me, too, man." Latham hurried toward his truck as the baby let out a wail so shrill that Cam was surprised the car windows didn't shatter.

Cam rounded the corner into the backyard and once again was struck by the sight. There were kids and adults of all ages, from babies to one guy who looked like he must be eighty. The old guy was playing beanbag toss with a little girl who looked to be around eight or nine.

He caught sight of Eleanor in the playhouse with another little girl. Penny, maybe? He was usually so good with names, but there were just so many of them.

A bunch of boys were shooting hoops on the basketball court and he had a moment of guilt because he hadn't made it over to throw the ball with Deke this week. There were a few more kids down by the pond digging in the mud. He wondered how Claire would deal with that, but when he looked around, he spotted her rocking in the porch swing with a fat black puppy in her lap.

His puppy.

He took the stairs up to the back porch and greeted Claire. "Looks like you have a new friend."

"She's so sweet, Cam. I want one, but Joe would literally kill me. One of the goats is pregnant and he's so grumpy about it."

Cam laughed. "I'm looking for Jules. She had the kids last night and I apparently slept straight through church and lunch."

"I know how that feels. There's only so long you can go without sleep before your body gives out." Claire had a serene look on her face, but her eyes never stopped moving, following the kids in the yard. "Jules is in the kitchen with the others. Go on in."

Cam didn't really want to interrupt a "sibling pow-wow," as Latham had put it, but he pulled open the screen door and stepped into the room. Four sets of blue eyes swung around. "I, uh, just wanted to let Jules know I was here. I can go back out and watch the kids, if you want me to."

"It's okay—Latham's aunt Dot is watching them. Come on in. We're just getting started." Jules sat at the end of the table with an untouched mug of coffee in front of her. She had deep circles under her eyes and barely looked like herself. Her tightly strung tension was the antithesis of Claire's calm.

Cam took one of the stools next to the huge island. It was a kitchen made for a big family, with lots of stools at the bar, a family-size farm table and a sitting area with a couch facing a huge fireplace.

Joe cleared his throat. "Before we start, we need to agree that for the purposes of this conversation, we're all happy for Mom and we think it's great that she's on her honeymoon with—" he rubbed his hand along his stubbly jawline "—with Mickey."

"We *are* all happy for Mom. But her leaving the café and expecting Jules to just run it, along with everything else going on? That wasn't right." Wynn was apparently the outspoken one.

"There's one thing y'all should probably know before we get started." Jules walked over to the bar stool where she'd left her bag and pulled out a sheaf of papers, handing it over the table to Wynn.

Wynn glanced at the papers, looked up at Jules, frowned, and squinted at the small print again. "This is the deed. Mom signed the café over to you. Did she ask you before she put all this in your name?"

"No. But what was I going to say? I mean, come on. It's not like I really had a choice. Mom thought she was giving me this amazing gift. I couldn't exactly shove it back in her face."

Wynn tapped a manicured finger on the reclaimed-wood table and nodded at Cam. "In the meantime, neither of you is sleeping and you have two kids who really need your attention right now."

Ash leaned back in his seat, his arm stretched out across the back of the chair next to him. "We need to pitch in and help, Jules. This is too much for you to handle. It would be too much for any one of us to handle. So, I'm off work on Wednesday afternoons. I usually have Levi, but I can figure something out."

Joe nodded. "I'm sure there's at least one day a week when I can break away."

"Or…" Jules looked down at the table. "We can put a sign on the door that they're on their honeymoon and close the café."

Cam wasn't expecting that, and by the way the others swiveled to look at her, they weren't, either.

The silence stretched.

She shrugged and looked from one sibling to another. "I can't do it. Won't do it. Cam and I are stretched as thin as we can stretch. I didn't see the girls for five days straight last week."

Joe gave a single definitive nod. "That settles it, then."

Wynn grabbed her hand. "No one could do it, Jules. It's all right."

A tear hung precariously on Jules's lower lashes. Cam stared at it in stupefaction. He didn't know Jules well, but he knew her well enough to know she didn't admit defeat.

"I'm not saying it's going to be closed forever, but for now, it's what I need to do. Cam was a trouper this week, but the girls need both of us." Jules swallowed hard and her voice broke. "Mom's going to be so disappointed in me."

"No. She's not." Cam slid off the stool before he even knew he was planning to move. He stood behind Jules and slid his hands over her shoulders. "She loves you and choosing to do this is not the easy choice."

"Cam's right. Don't worry about Mom." Ash glanced down at his phone as it buzzed in his hand. "And I've gotta run. I'm on call this weekend. But, Jules, listen. You painted my exam rooms when I was getting ready to open the practice and was too in debt to pay someone to do it. You've done the same kind of thing for all of us. Whatever you need, I'm here for it."

Her shoulders trembled underneath Cam's fingers.

"Thank you. All of you. I don't even know what to say."

"Say you'll call when you need help." Joe pushed away from the table. "I've gotta get going, too."

"I'm proud of you, sis. Life's beat you down a bit lately, but instead of letting it get to you, you're punching it in the mouth and taking charge. I wouldn't expect anything else." Wynn met Cam's eyes before stepping outside and letting the screen door slam behind her.

Cam stood in the same place behind Jules for a minute, quiet falling around them. Random shouts and squeals of laughter from the backyard filtered in through the open windows, along with the spring breeze.

Finally, she sighed. "The more we talked about what to do, the more I knew I couldn't do it. I just don't know where to go from here."

She stood and faced him, traces of her inner struggle still on her face, and Cam wondered if this was the first time he'd truly seen her, without a plan, without the walls that she had erected so carefully to protect herself. "We'll figure it out, Jules. Together. As long as we're not going in two different directions, it's gonna be okay."

He hesitated—because despite everything, he didn't know if he had the right—then pulled her into his arms, anyway, and with her head nestled just under his chin, held her. "I promise we'll make it okay."

It was still new—this fledgling relationship they were building. Somewhere in the back of his mind he'd wondered how long Jules thought this marriage was going to last. Was it just a temporary fix until custody of the girls was assured? Was it forever? Did she even know?

For today, anyway, she was in his arms. And that would have to be enough.

Chapter Eight

Jules piped frosting into her signature swirl on a row of cupcakes. The aroma that wafted toward her was classic birthday cake, and with its cotton candy–blue frosting and multicolored sprinkles, this cupcake was a bestseller in the bakery. And with each one she frosted, she could feel her blood pressure returning to normal.

At the early-morning staff meeting, she'd filled her employees in on the new plan. With the café temporarily closed, April would be opening up the bakery for now. Lanna was moving over from the Hilltop to work the afternoon-to-evening shift at the bakery, and Jules would come in midday while the girls were at day care. A couple of the part-timers from the café would be filling in on the weekends.

Not one person complained about the changes, which told her they'd all been fully aware of how awful things were last week.

Heat rose in her face just thinking about it. What a tumble she'd taken from perfection—and what a relief today to be able to focus on the bakery. Well, the bakery, her two babies, a new husband, a waterlogged house that had taken the water mitigators weeks to dry out and the mother of all stressors—a custody battle.

She couldn't think about any of that too much or she couldn't breathe.

"Hey, sis." Wynn stepped through the door into the kitchen, wearing a suit and heels, her long blond hair corralled into a sleek ponytail. "I just stopped by to make sure you were okay. Yesterday, you looked like you were ready to keel over. So, how are you?"

"Better." Jules went back to her cupcakes. "A little embarrassed that I couldn't handle the pressure."

"It's not worth killing yourself just so you meet everyone else's expectations."

"It's not everyone else's expectations that are the problem." Jules valued excellence. It was why every single one of her cupcakes had the exact same swirl, why she liked the kitchen to be sparkling every night before she went to bed. Why she did a million other things she did. And she was rationalizing again. "I'm learning. Give me time."

"I will if you give me one of those cupcakes to take back to the office."

Jules laughed. "Take one for Garrett, too."

"Speaking of Garrett, he asked me to give this to you." Wynn pulled an envelope out of her bag. "He said he emailed it to you, also."

"Give me that." Jules dropped the piping bag as her stomach bottomed out. So much for not thinking about it. If Garrett was sending her something, it had to do with custody of the girls. She ripped open the envelope and pulled out a piece of paper. "It's an order from the judge, but I don't know what it means."

Wynn took the paper and skimmed it. "Looks like the judge issued an order assigning a guardian ad litem, a lawyer to represent Emma and Eleanor's best interests. That's usually a good thing, hon. Don't worry."

"I need to tell Cam about this. You sticking around?"

"Nope. I have court this afternoon, hence the killer suit, so I'm taking my cupcakes to-go."

"Thanks for bringing that by. I'll see you later." Jules grabbed her phone from the desk in her office, realizing as she did that she'd left it on Silent after her staff meeting this morning. *Oh, no.* She had two missed calls from the preschool and one from Cam.

She dialed the preschool back first. "This is Jules Shee—Quinn. Jules Quinn. You called me a little while ago?"

There was some shuffling and what sounded like someone slamming the phone on the desk before the director picked up the line. "Hey, Jules. It's Caroline. Emma had a fever this morning, so we were calling you to come and pick her up. We were able to get Mr. Quinn on the phone, though, and he picked her up around forty-five minutes ago."

"Thank you." She hung up the phone. Emma had been fussy for the past few days, but Jules and Cam both thought it was just teething. Clearly, her parenting skills were on point. Her stomach sinking, she scrolled through her missed texts until she saw the one from Cam: I've got Emma. Taking her to see Ash. Don't worry—I've got this.

Of course she was going to worry. Jules grabbed her purse from the back of her office chair and started for the door, stopping briefly to tell April she was leaving before hitting the street at a run. Finishing the cupcakes didn't matter.

Nothing did when stacked against the fact that her baby was sick.

Cam paced the floor in the pediatrician's office with a red-faced, fussy Emma, his heart racing. He felt marginally better now that he was actually in the doctor's office. When he'd picked Emma up at day care, he'd felt a little bit like he was carrying a ticking time bomb that could go off at any minute.

There were any number of horrible things that could happen to a kid with a fever, the least of which was projectile vomiting, something that Cam knew for a fact he wasn't at all prepared for.

A soft knock at the door preceded Ash, wearing a crisp white coat and a startlingly red polka-dot bow tie. "I wasn't expecting to see you two again so soon after our family lunch yesterday. It says here that Emma has a fever. Any details?"

"They called me from day care to come and pick her up. She's been really out of sorts for a few days, but she's had her hand in her mouth all the time. I thought she was teething."

"Okay, let's take a look. You can keep holding her. She'll probably like that better." Ash rubbed his stethoscope in his opposite palm for a minute, warming it before placing it on Emma's little bare back. He moved it around, a look of concentration on his face. "Her lungs sound good. Let's look in her ears while you're holding her. Just hold her head on your shoulder— yep, just like that."

Ash looked in Emma's ear. "That one looks a tiny bit red. Let's see the other side."

Cam switched Emma to his other shoulder and gently held her head while Ash looked in the other ear.

"Gross. Well, I think we found the culprit for the fever. That one's definitely infected. Okay, you can lay her down on the table."

Infected? Cam's stomach sank. "So she has an ear infection? She hasn't been herself, but I just thought she was teething. No wonder she was so hard to calm."

Ash looked up and apparently caught a glimpse of Cam's face, because he straightened, his hand on Emma's belly. "Okay, first of all, it's entirely possible that this started as teething, so stop beating yourself up about that. Second, what you're feeling is regular old parent guilt and you're going to have to put it aside. You're not a bad dad because you missed an ear infection."

Cam barely heard the rest of Ash's pep talk because his attention snagged on the word *parent*. What he was feeling was *parent* guilt, *dad* guilt. The thought was a revelation.

"Okay, you can get her dressed now." Ash waited until Cam had his hands on Emma before turning to the counter, talking as he typed. "I'm going to send a prescription to the pharmacy for an antibiotic, affectionately known to parents of young children as 'the pink stuff.' The pharmacist will give you a syringe to dose it and the instructions will be on the bottle."

He turned around and faced Cam, his arms crossed. "So, what's the deal with my sister?"

Cam, his fingers fumbling on the snaps of Emma's sleeper, looked up. "What?"

"It just seems that y'all got married awfully fast. I could tell yesterday that you care about her."

Cam lifted Emma to his shoulder. "Ah...yes. Yes, I care about her."

"Good. Because if you break her heart, I'll personally make sure you're sorry."

"Ash? Cam? Are you in there?" The door to the exam room flew open and Jules rushed in. She promptly scooped Emma into her arms, the loose legs of the sleeper flapping.

Cam didn't even try to speak. There was no point in trying to get between Jules and Emma.

"Oh, baby, I'm so sorry you're feeling bad." She rubbed Emma's head and turned on Ash. "Is she okay? Why does she have a fever?"

"She's going to be fine, Jules." Ash put his arm around his sister and squeezed. "Just a simple ear infection. I'll let Cam tell you about it. I've got to keep moving."

The door closed behind him, leaving Cam and Jules in the exam room with Emma, who was whiny and sleepy. He put his hand on Emma's tiny back. "Ash sent a prescription to the pharmacy. She'll be good as new in a few days."

"I feel so bad."

"Me, too. But according to your brother, that's just your average parent guilt and we need to get used to it." Cam gathered the diaper bag and blanket. Jules was standing in the open door now, her mouth hanging open. He had a moment of sympathy for her, considering he'd had the exact same feeling a few minutes ago when Ash first said it to him.

"Jules."

She looked at him, her eyes wide, and he smiled at her. "I'll take her home so you can get back to work."

"No, I'm not going back. I want to be with Emma when she's sick."

Emma's cries had turned to legitimate screaming, the kind where her face turned purple and she had to pause for air. Cam wasn't sure if it was her ear or if she was just over the whole doctor thing, but either way he wasn't arguing with Jules. He followed her out the front door. "Let's get Em in the car and see if that calms her down. And maybe we should get some fever reducer at the drugstore."

He slid into the driver's seat while Jules snapped Emma into the car seat and gave her a pacifier. He was pretty sure that wouldn't last, but at least the volume of the crying went down a little. Jules opened the passenger-side door. "Hey, don't forget your car is across the street at the bakery."

"Come on. Start the car. She always goes to sleep in the car seat."

Cam turned the key in the ignition and, sure enough, as the motor started humming, Emma's pacifier-muffled cries started to fade.

Jules looked over at him. "It's like the magic bullet. The only problem is you can't stop."

Cam looked down. He had a full tank of gas and a load of your average dad guilt for missing that Emma had an ear infection. So he put the car in Drive.

Jules pointed to a small indentation in the trees. "Here. Turn here!"

He whipped the wheel to the side and turned onto an overgrown dirt road. As they bounced over the grooved track, Jules glanced back to make sure Emma was still sleeping. So far so good. She'd fallen asleep as they pulled into their driveway, and because they knew better, they backed out again and kept driving.

"And how does getting stuck in the middle of nowhere help us out this afternoon?" Cam's voice was dry.

She shot him a look. "Trust me."

He laughed, his eyes on the narrow trail ahead of them. "Apparently, I do. With my whole life."

Her breath caught in surprise, but in a way, he was right. And she was trusting him just as much, which explained why they were both on tenterhooks all the time. It was really hard handing your heart—handing your life—into the hands of someone you barely knew, even if that person happened to be your spouse.

They drove for another minute, bouncing over the ruts in the rarely used road. She leaned forward. "Just a little farther."

A few seconds later, they broke through the trees into a clearing. Light speared through the clouds, sparkling on the river below.

Jules sat back with a smile as Cam let the car roll to a stop.

He put the vehicle in Park, letting out a low whistle. "Remind me not to question your sense of direction in the future. This is spectacular."

She unlatched her seat belt and reached down to the floor, where she'd left the bag from the drugstore. "When I ran in to check on the prescription, I picked up a little something."

From the bag, she pulled out two pints of ice cream

and a package of plastic spoons. "I feel like we deserve this. It's been a whale of a two weeks."

He laughed. "That's about the truest thing I've ever heard."

She checked on Emma again. The infant pain reliever they got at the pharmacy must've kicked in because for the first time in several days, she was sleeping soundly. It was a relief, in a way, to know something was wrong and they could fix it.

Jules tucked her feet underneath her and took a bite of her ice cream. As it melted in her mouth and the silence settled in the car, she could feel the tension doing the same. In the distance a barge chugged toward them, the powerful engines of the towboat pushing the huge craft upriver against the current.

That was the way she felt. Like the past couple months since her friend died she had been here alone, pushing against the current. Until Cam came along and she wasn't doing it alone anymore. It was still hard, but the problem with the current didn't seem so insurmountable.

The undercurrent…now, that was another story. She could almost hear the low hum in the silence between them. The sound of all the unspoken…stuff between her and Cam.

She cleared her throat. "I know you didn't expect to take on the girls, me, my messy life. It hasn't been easy on you, I know that."

He was quiet, taking a couple of bites of ice cream, his eyes on the river, before responding. "I'm not gonna lie—it hasn't been a walk in the park. But it hasn't been easy on you, either. You took in two grieving kids, even if they didn't understand what they were grieving for, when you were devastated yourself."

"I haven't even had time to really process Glory's death. It seems like this black hole that I have to keep stepping around in my mind because I don't want to fall into it."

Cam's eyes were on the barge crossing in front of them on the river. "I get that. I have a few of those places in my mind I don't want to visit. Regardless, you've handled it."

"Maybe. I haven't handled any of it very well, though." She shook her head. "The café? I can't even. I need to figure out a way I can balance everything with our family."

Our family. She gulped and barreled on, not wanting to think about the consequences of that statement. "To be honest, I was surprised no one objected to closing the café, even temporarily. We all have more than a little sentimental attachment to the place."

"Did you know your mom used to let me sweep up after school so I could get a doughnut on my way home?"

She smiled. "I didn't know that, but I'm not surprised."

"She always had a way with the misfits. When I walked into the café after being gone for fifteen years, it was like I'd just walked out last week. I have a sentimental attachment to the Hilltop, too. I bet everyone in town does, which is why they would still come even if you decided to do something completely different with it."

"I bet when you rolled into town that day, you didn't expect to be married a week later."

"No. That's one even a fiction writer couldn't dream up. I'm not sorry, though."

"You sound surprised."

"Aren't you?" He turned toward her and brushed a flyaway curl from her face, his hand trembling a little bit. "Are you that much of an optimist? That when you came up with that idea, you were like, 'Oh, yeah, we'll go with the easy plan.'"

She laughed quietly and wrenched her gaze away from his long mesmerizing fingers. "You know better than that. That was the plan of a desperate realist."

"Last week was completely awful."

She winced. "I know. I'm sorry."

"It's not your fault. I just know the girls missed you. *I* missed you. Missed this. Sitting, talking nonsense about our day."

She looked back at him then and his eyes were steady on hers, full of dark emotion.

He sighed, shrugged a little. "I was angry for so long after I left Red Hill Springs, and when the anger burned out, there was just…nothing. I've never had this, Jules. Never had anyone to share life with, not like this."

Her throat ached with emotion. This was an arrangement, a contract, so to speak. This wasn't a romance. It wasn't even meant to last.

"This isn't real," she whispered, her eyes still locked on his. But all those what-ifs—the ones she kept pushing away in the middle of the night—wouldn't leave her alone. What if it could be real? What if she leaned into this relationship?

Leaned into him?

In the back seat, Emma squirmed and whimpered.

Cam held her gaze for another long second. Then he smiled, the emotion vanishing from his face. "No, you're right. We should probably go. Emma's medicine is ready by now and we need to pick Eleanor up."

As he put the car in gear, she stared out the window at the sparkling river. Going against the current was difficult. More difficult than just going with the flow of the water. Unlikely, even.

But still...

That towboat had been straining to push a barge full of cargo up the river. The waves were choppy and the trip upriver would always be challenging. And yet the pilot was still able to safely navigate to where he wanted to go.

She glanced over at Cam's handsome profile—his strong jaw spoke to the strong character underneath. She wasn't sure there was anything safe about this relationship with Cam.

Especially not her heart.

Chapter Nine

The text had said to meet Jules at the bakery after dropping the girls off at day care. Jules's assistant, April, had told Cam that she was next door at the café. The lights were off, but the door was unlocked. He pushed it open, smiling a little at the jingle of the bells hanging on the handle.

In the darkened room, with no patrons, the café looked a little worn and sad. The benches in the booths were aging and cracked. The air today wasn't filled with the aroma of fresh blueberry pancakes and bacon, and it seemed stale and heavy.

Jules looked up from where she was sitting at a back booth. Sunlight poured through the adjacent window, making her blond hair glow like a halo. He slid onto the bench across from her. The table was covered with papers. Drawings, to be more precise. "What's this about?"

She flattened one hand on the table, a pencil still wedged underneath her index finger, and gestured with the other. "Okay. Don't talk until I'm done, because I want you to hear the whole thing before you make a judgment. But something you said yesterday got me thinking."

"Yeah? What did I say?" That one drawing on top looked like a long glass bakery counter. Was she thinking of expanding the bakery into the café?

He looked up to find her patiently waiting for his attention. "Sorry. Continue."

She went on. "When I was feeding Emma a bottle in the middle of the night last night, I remembered that you said something about how people would come to the café even if I did something completely different with it."

He narrowed his eyes. "Yes…"

She lifted a finger and he closed his mouth. "So part of what drives me crazy about the café is that I'm not good at running it. I don't have control over the menu or really even the quality of food because it's not my expertise. *But*…if I create a menu that combines my love of baking with quality local ingredients, I think I could really get excited about that."

"Okay, so far I like this idea."

She slid a piece of paper across the table—the drawing he'd been trying to decipher. "So basically, what I'm thinking is we combine the bakery and the café. We have this long glass case, and at one end it's a bakery case and the other end is where you order."

He nodded. "I can see it."

"We'll open for breakfast and lunch, serve bakery items, pastries and such, but we'll also serve a few specialty items like French toast for breakfast and hand-carved sandwiches or quiche, maybe, for lunch. With me so far?"

"It sounds awesome. I want some French toast right now."

Jules laughed. "I'm sure you'll get the chance. I have to test the menu items on someone. Which brings me to my last point. I'll create the menu and we'll hire someone to run the place for the day-to-day."

"I think it's a fantastic... Wait." He paused, replaying the conversation in his head. "You said *we*. *We* open for breakfast and lunch. *We* hire someone to run the place."

She tapped her pencil on the table, looking down, her eyes—and her feelings—hidden. "Truth is, Cam, I need an investor. I can't afford to do this on my own."

"So it's about the money. That's why you asked me here?"

"No!" She met his eyes across the table now, her gaze intense and direct. "No. Or at least not completely. It would be a big project in the short run, but in the long run, doing this would free me up to do what I love—be the creative force behind an innovative menu *and* spend time with you and the kids."

"Okay."

She closed her eyes, then tilted her head and opened one a crack, looking at him through a veil of lashes. "Okay...yes?"

He laughed. "Okay, yes. But I'm not doing it as a favor. This is a sound investment."

Jules pulled him to his feet and threw her arms around his neck. He closed his arms around her. Oh, she was remarkable. Smart, creative, driven, unshakable.

No wonder his plan—the one to delude himself into believing he was marrying her solely to protect the girls—was failing. He let her slide back to the floor. "I do have one condition, though."

"What is it?"

"We go on a date. A *real* date, with a babysitter and everything. We can ask Joe's daughter, Amelia."

She caught her bottom lip between her teeth as she studied his face. "A date."

Cam grinned. "Yep. You know the concept. We dress up. Have food that neither of us cooked. Do something fun… A date."

Shoving him gently, she laughed. "I'll agree to dessert Wednesday night after we get the kids to bed."

Resilience. That was the word for what he admired about her so much. Every time life dealt her a blow, she stood back up and faced it down with heart and brains. Grit.

He was so toast.

"The girls are asleep, but sometimes Eleanor has nightmares. If that happens, it helps to make her some warm milk and let her have a few minutes before you try to put her back to bed."

Amelia, Jules's fourteen-year-old niece, stuck her cell phone in the back pocket of her skinny jeans, jeans that looked like they'd been cut and burned and dragged behind an 18-wheeler. "Okay, got it. No problem."

"And Emma's had an ear infection. She's been on medicine for a couple of days, but she's been getting up for a bottle again. There are three in the refrigerator if you need them."

"Emma might need a bottle. Check." Amelia looked

around the large kitchen and peered into the living room. "This place is lit. Is there a pool?"

"A pool?" Jules looked at her blankly. "Yes, there's a pool."

"Cool. This summer when I come to babysit, I can take the girls swimming."

The thought of both girls in the pool, or even near the pool, without Jules there was absolutely horrifying. "Um, sure. That sounds good. So, you have our numbers if you need anything. If you have any questions about anything at all..."

Cam put one hand on the small of Jules's back and slid his other hand down her arm to link his fingers with hers, then slowly backed toward the door, dragging her along with him. "Jules, Amelia has more experience with little kids and babies than both of us combined."

Jules turned to face him, her fingers still entwined with his. "Right."

He smiled over her shoulder at Amelia. "We'll be just down in the barn if you need us."

"The barn? Really?" Jules looked down at the dress he'd suggested she wear and the high heels she'd chosen at the last minute. This was, after all, a date. That was apparently going to be in a barn.

Guiding her with the firm pressure of his hand at her back, Cam led her through the French doors and onto the wide deck. "I knew you'd be worried about leaving them. This way, we get our date and you can rest easy about the girls."

Tears pricked her eyes. She blinked them back in surprise. She wasn't a crier. She'd figured out, growing up the youngest of four, that tears only made you vulnerable, so she'd learned to hide them.

As they crossed the yard, the first sprinkles of a spring rain splashed down. His fingers tightened around the curve of her waist, sending little sparks of awareness through her. He paused to slide open the door to the barn and she walked in ahead of him. This space was no ordinary shelter for animals on a normal day, with its beautiful, high-arching wood beams, but tonight…

It was magical.

In the center of the large room, she spun, trying to take it all in. The lights were low, twinkle lights crisscrossing from one side of the rafters to the other. At the far end, near the open door, a table was set with china, crystal and flowers.

She sought him out. "Cam, I don't know what to say. This is amazing."

He advanced slowly toward her, devastating to her equilibrium in his khaki slacks, crisp white shirt and perfectly tailored jacket. He had one hand in his pants pocket, so effortlessly masculine that had she been any less practical, it's possible she would've swooned.

Cam pulled his hand out of his pocket, holding a tiny remote. He clicked it and some smooth jazz filled the room from speakers she couldn't even see.

"We didn't get a first dance at our wedding. So I thought…" He laughed a little. "Honestly, I'm not sure what I thought, but I wanted you to have a first dance."

She meant to move, to reach for his outstretched hands, but she could only stand and stare and wonder that he'd pulled off something so incredibly sweet. For her.

Cam smiled, his dimple deepening with a hint of insecurity, but he didn't hesitate. He reached for her hand and slowly drew her toward him as the music surrounded them.

For a moment, he swayed gently with her, holding her as carefully as if *she* were fine china. Then he lifted her hand, leading her into a spin, and she laughed before he caught her in his arms again.

The clean, fresh smell of rain filled the barn. With the sound of the raindrops on the roof, the music and the lights, she felt like they were the only two people in the world.

It was sweet. *He* was sweet. She smiled up at him and the tenderness she saw in his eyes almost undid her. She'd been so independent her whole life, so driven, that people just expected her to not need anything. But Cam didn't see that hard outer shell she showed to the world—he saw her.

And it was such a relief not to have to hide. She closed her eyes, laying her head on his chest as he spun them around the room. He hummed a little and she could feel the deep timbre of his voice rumble in his chest.

"Sometimes I catch a glimpse of you walking through the house with one of the girls and I wonder who you are for a minute." He murmured in her ear, tucking her hand between them. "And when I remember, I'm blown away that you're my wife."

Releasing her hands, he cupped her face in his palms and brushed the gentlest kiss she could imagine across her lips. One shaky breath in and he closed his eyes, exploring the contours of her face, the curve of her neck, with his strong, clever fingers.

He cinched his arm around her waist and pulled her closer, deepening the kiss.

She wanted to melt into him, to lose all the worry, all the heartache and stress, to forget about everything except for Cam. It would be so easy—so easy to forget it wasn't really real.

He broke the kiss. "Jules, I…I can't do this. I'm sorry."

Jules opened her eyes, her thoughts scrambling as fear rushed in.

She took a step back, panic rising in her chest as she silently berated herself for letting it go this far. Turning away from him, she ran for the door, stopping only to tip her shoes off.

In her mind was a constant running refrain: *What have I done?*

"Jules!" He closed the distance between them as she threw a frantic glance out at the pouring rain. "Jules, wait. Please."

He was a famous author. A world traveler. He was known for staying only a few months in one place before going on to the next adventure. Just how reckless had she been?

When she'd asked him to marry her, her only worry had been for the girls' little hearts.

She hadn't even spared a thought for her own.

Chapter Ten

"Jules…wait. Please." Cam held out his hands. "Please."

From the barn door, Jules looked back at him, but her muscles were tensed, ready to run.

He walked slowly toward her, despite the very real fear that she would turn away from him. He could see the panic in her eyes. In a way, he even understood it.

"Cam, I don't—I'm—I don't even—" She closed her eyes, took a deep breath and opened them again, still not reaching for his hand. "We can talk. We can't touch. I can't think when you're touching me."

He nearly smiled, but thought better of it. "There's a spot in the loft where you can look out over the pond. Can we just go sit?"

"Yes."

At the top of the stairs was the caretaker's apartment Cam had made into his office. He opened the door and let Jules go in ahead of him. She circled the studio apartment, something he did often himself as he was puzzling out a difficult scene. She trailed her finger down the granite countertop in the tiny kitchen where he kept his coffeepot. "This is a great office."

"It is." He pulled open a set of double doors and she followed him out onto a small balcony. Though the downpour had slowed, raindrops still tapped haphazardly on the metal roof. Two chairs were tucked into the small space. He held one for her and then took the other.

Even in the relative darkness, it was possible to see the property stretched out before them, small glimmers and sparks on the pond from the lights of the house, and beyond the pasture, the darker gray green of the woods. It was beautiful and peaceful here, despite the woman beside him who had the ability to destroy his calm in about two seconds flat.

In fact, if he was being honest with himself, she'd flattened him with his first glimpse of her and he'd been trying to find his footing ever since. Which brought him, he guessed, to this conversation in which he had to lay bare all of his miserable past—because while he might know who he was kissing, she most certainly did not.

He'd hoped he would have a few more weeks before he had to have this conversation with Jules. Or, if he was brutally honest, maybe he'd hoped to never have it. But she needed to know—he wasn't the gallant Uncle Cam here to save the girls.

Far from it.

Cam stared at a flicker of light in the distance. "I have a story to tell you."

"I hope you're as good with telling a story as you are writing them."

He glanced at her in surprise. "You've read one of my books?"

Her skin was dewy from the humidity, her hair curling in ringlets around her face, light from the open doorway glimmering in the golden strands. Faint pink stained her cheeks. "I haven't had time to read all of them, but I read the one set in Romania."

He was flattered and touched, and somehow, the fact that she'd read one of his books made this conversation even harder. "This isn't a story about an adventure. Although I guess maybe you could consider it a prequel."

He had a vivid imagination, a great skill for a writer, not so great when you had the kind of toxic memories he carried. As he wondered where to start with Jules, he could feel the hot, close walls of that little house where he'd lived with his mother and step-father and Glory, smell the sour, fetid scent of the ever-present empty bottles.

"I wanted to play football." It was as good a place to start as any. He narrowed his eyes against the wave of longing that rushed over him. He could taste the bitterness he'd felt in those days, scraping a life from the ruin of his family.

It was then he'd learned to leave that squalid little house behind and pretend to be someone else, someone better, someone who fitted in. "I tried out for the team, but I needed money for cleats. You know, opportunities are supposed to be equal for kids in school, but they're not. Kids who don't have money don't get to play sports."

She frowned and he wondered what she was thinking. He wanted to ask her, but if he did, he wasn't sure he could come back to the rest of it. He took a deep breath and barreled on.

"I'd been saving up but I still needed ten bucks. When I left for school that morning, my stepfather was passed out on the couch. Beside him, on the scratched-up end table, was some wadded-up cash. I didn't even think, Jules. I grabbed the cash, took it in my room and hid it in the mayonnaise jar with the rest of the money I'd been saving."

His gaze was on the pond, but instead he was seeing the jar with all the money he'd saved, the desperate hope he'd felt that maybe he'd finally get something he wanted. "When I got home from school, he was sitting on the couch, the jar open in front of him on the coffee table. He wanted me to admit that I'd stolen from him."

She sucked in a small, quick breath.

"I thought about lying, but I didn't. I just shrugged, like *yeah, whatever.* So he backhanded me and called me a worthless—well, let's just say he called me a derogatory name no kid should ever hear." Cam had felt searing anger when he'd heard the word, but he hadn't felt shame until he looked to his mother to defend him and she turned away. His lip twitched, his eyes closing against the memory, fingers going to the scar. "He laid open the skin on my cheekbone, but that's not what hurt the worst. I wanted my mom to stop him, to stand up for me, but he kicked me out, and she didn't say a word."

"Cam." Jules reached for his hand and her touch was enough to break the grip of the past, but it couldn't erase the hollowness he felt. He opened his eyes.

"So, the thing is, Jules, you're right to be afraid

of me. You're right to want to run. It's a total fluke I ended up with the career I have now. I've done some terrible things to survive." Things that made him break out in a sick, cold sweat when he thought about them.

"Those things weren't your fault, Cam. You were just a kid."

"You don't know, Jules. You don't even know the half of it." He interrupted her because she just didn't get it. There were more things, *worse* things…

"Where did you go when you left Red Hill Springs?"

"I hitched a ride out of town. It took some time but I ended up in New York, in Brooklyn, where I met Ya-ya. She's the one who taught me how to make pad thai. She gave me a Bible and a job, in that order." He smiled, the pungent, competing aromas of lemongrass, kaffir lime and coriander in his memory now, powerful because to him they smelled like survival.

Like hope.

"She was a lifeline. I was so angry and so focused on my own pain I couldn't see anyone else. She bought my first plane ticket and sent me to visit her family in Thailand. And…I learned the world didn't revolve around me. After that I was hooked. I would work, earn enough money to go somewhere for a few months, work some more, go somewhere else. I honestly never thought I'd come back to Red Hill Springs."

"I can't imagine how hard it was even to cross the city limits."

She had no idea how much he'd wanted to turn around and go the other way, get on a plane, go back to Morocco and put this place as far out of his mind as he could.

But Emma and Eleanor needed him. And, it turned out, he needed them.

"I've been a lot of things to a lot of people," he said slowly. "But I've never had a home. When I walked into this house for the first time, I wanted it, but I didn't just want the house. I wanted a life. A home. I wanted a family. Kids cartwheeling on the lawn and fishing in the pond. I'm not proud, Jules, but somewhere inside I guess I felt like if I had all the things I dreamed about my whole childhood that I'd know I really made it out of there."

He paused. "And suddenly, even though I knew I didn't deserve it, there was a way for me to have it all."

And he'd tried to make it work, tried to make that enough. But he was falling for her and she deserved so much better than the kid even a mother couldn't love.

Jules was trembling. "So you took the deal."

"I took the deal."

Jules looked over at Cam's stoic face. He'd finished baring his past to her, and now he looked like he could've been carved out of stone. He deserved so much better than he'd gotten from his parents. And so much better than a sham of a marriage that only looked like a dream coming true.

He deserved the real thing. And the saddest part of all was he didn't even know it. "Oh, Cam. You are worthy of so much more than this."

Her heart felt like it might shatter into a million pieces and she was so mad at herself. It wasn't like she hadn't known that going on a date with him and dancing and kissing were a bad idea. She just hadn't known *how* bad an idea they were.

She also hadn't known he'd had a plan from the beginning and was, for lack of a better metaphor, checking the boxes, creating a family for himself. But she'd known it wasn't real, so if all of this was painful… well, it wasn't as painful as what Cam had endured, and it was her own stinking fault.

With the slowing of the rain came a drop in the temperature. Jules shivered.

He moved immediately, holding out his hand to help her to her feet. "Come on, it's getting cold out here. Let's go back to the house."

She put her hand in his, but when he pulled her to her feet, he didn't let go. He drew her into his office and dragged a cashmere throw from the couch, wrapping it around her shoulders. She sighed and clasped the soft fabric closer. He was still taking care of her.

A huge part of her wanted to take him in her arms and tell him it was all going to be okay, but she couldn't. She didn't have the right, because they weren't a couple and he didn't love her. He hadn't even pretended to love her. He loved the *idea* of her—that was totally different.

"What you did tonight was lovely. No one's ever done anything like that for me before…but it can't happen again."

He looked shattered and she had to remind herself that she couldn't go to him. She couldn't remind him that he was important to her. "So here's the deal. We got married for the girls and we'll stay married for the girls, but we're not a couple. We have to agree…no more quiet talks. No more dates. No more kissing." She paused. "*Especially* no more kissing."

"Agreed." As her teeth threatened to chatter, he

tugged the throw closer around her. "We're not a couple."

There was so much more she wanted to say, but she needed some distance from him. She needed to think through the crazy gamut of emotions she'd run tonight. She needed to step back, have a plan. She sighed wearily. "We need to get back."

He went down the stairs first, steadying her as she stepped onto the floor of the barn, and turning off the lights and music as they left. She didn't bother with her shoes. The heels would've sunk into the rain-softened lawn, anyway. When they reached the house, she said, "I'll take Amelia home. I just want to change clothes."

From upstairs in the bedroom, Jules could hear the murmur of Cam's deep voice and Amelia's quicker, bouncier reply. Jules threw on a sweatshirt and yoga pants, grabbed her tennis shoes and stopped just outside the door to the kitchen to slide them on.

"So, your dad mentioned that he moved back to town a couple of years ago. Where'd you guys move from?"

Jules went still, her hand creeping up to cover her mouth. He didn't know.

"I'd actually never met my dad when I moved here. My mom dropped me off on my grandma's doorstep with a backpack and a note. How about you?"

There was a moment of silence where Jules could imagine Cam trying to catch up with this turn in the conversation. She heard one of the kitchen chairs pull out and, when she peeked around the corner, she saw Amelia sitting at the table, chin in hand.

"I got kicked out by my mom and stepdad when I

was fifteen. Never met my dad at all, so you've got me beat there." Cam went to the pantry, got a package of cookies and tossed them on the table before dropping into the chair across from her. "So, you lived with your mom. Never met your dad. Got dropped off at…Bertie's house with a note. That sum it up?"

"Don't forget the backpack of clothes I'd outgrown two years before," she said matter-of-factly. "My dad handled it pretty good. I kind of hated him, though."

"Really?" Cam took a cookie and shoved the package toward her. "Oreo?"

Amelia took one of the cookies and pulled the two chocolate sides apart, licking the frosting. "Yeah, but then we moved to the farm and Dad and Claire got married and I have, you know, a real family and food and stuff now."

Food and stuff.

Jules closed her eyes and whispered a prayer of thanks for her sweet niece. She took a deep breath and walked through the door. "Okay, you ready to go, Amelia?"

"Yep." Amelia got up from the table and pushed her chair in. "Thanks for the cookies, Uncle Cam."

He hesitated but smiled. "Anytime, kiddo."

"Go ahead to the car, Amelia. I'll be right there." Jules heard the garage door open as she stopped by the kitchen table. "I have something to say, Cam."

"Surprise." A tired smile kicked up one corner of his mouth, but he didn't look up, his eyes on the cookie in his hands as he turned the chocolate wafers around and around.

"What happened to you wasn't your fault. Your childhood, getting kicked out, none of it. You didn't cause it. It happened to you, but it was *not* your fault, any more than what happened to Amelia was hers."

"Thanks, Jules." When he looked up, his face was carefully blank, a look she hadn't seen since his first day or two here. He'd clearly retreated into his Cone of Distrust.

She drew in a breath, then sighed. "There's just one more thing. We may not be a couple, but you will always have a family."

He didn't say anything else. Once again, she wanted to reach out to him, but since she knew she couldn't, she followed Amelia to the car. The damp air hung around her like a wet blanket, and her heart felt heavy, too.

All the work they'd done in the past few weeks to create that thin bond between them had dissolved in the space of one conversation…under the weight of a broken childhood.

Chapter Eleven

Cam shoved away from his desk, staring at the blank screen of his computer. The blinking cursor taunted him with the futility of writing today. He'd played with the puppy until Pippi had collapsed in a boneless heap. He'd made coffee—twice. He'd ordered toys on the internet—for the kids and the dog. He was taking procrastination to a new level, but the fact was, he just couldn't concentrate.

His mind was on the conversation he'd had with Juliet last night. He hadn't slept at all, despite the exhaustion he still felt from the infamous "ear infection week." He'd never told anyone, not even Ya-ya, what happened that day he'd left home—what his stepfather had said and how his mother had turned away from him. And now he knew what it felt like to have your guts hanging out, life choices laid bare.

It was so much easier to get lost in a made-up story, a new character in a new place. His hero was about to paraglide off a mountain in Morocco to rescue his heroine in the latest adventure story. Cam, on the other hand, was about to make another cup of coffee.

He tossed his pencil down and watched it bounce off the desk and land somewhere behind his trash can.

"C'mon, Pippi. We're going to the house." The puppy tilted her head and obligingly loped to the stairs after Cam.

The storm of the night before had passed, leaving them with a crisp, cool spring day. The dog's attention was caught by a grasshopper, and she was halfway across the yard before Cam could close the barn door. At some point, he needed to clean up the remains of last night's date: the table, still laid with china and crystal, and the uneaten dessert, still in the cooler under the table.

Going on an actual date with Jules… It had been a good thought. Wasn't that what people said when they had good intentions, but the reality turned out to be a horrible mistake? Last night definitely hadn't gone as planned, but he was going to have to find a way to put it out of his mind and move forward. He and Jules had to work together for the girls.

Pippi ran ahead of him into the house when he opened the door to the kitchen, immediately sniffing under the high chair and nibbling the remains of whatever Emma had for breakfast. The espresso maker was on already, so Cam didn't have to wait for it to heat up, which foiled his plan to take as long as possible before he went back to not writing.

As the fragrant espresso streamed into his cup, he picked up an orange-yellow biscuit from a baking sheet and sniffed it. Sweet potato? He shrugged and slathered on some butter from the crock on the counter. He took a bite and looked at it in surprise. That was one delicious biscuit. Jules was upping her biscuit game for the new restaurant.

As the last of the steam from the espresso maker spurted into his mug, he realized he could hear the murmur of voices from the living room. Mug in hand, he strolled through the archway, expecting to find one of Juliet's siblings, and stumbled to a halt when he recognized the woman on the sofa.

She was older and life hadn't treated her well. Her face was grooved with time and hard living, but he had no problem recognizing her.

He looked at those eyes in the mirror every morning. "Hello, Mother."

She rose to her feet as he greeted her, her hand going to her chest. He acknowledged that she'd at least put a little bit of effort into her appearance. Her black hair, now streaked with gray, was still damp and combed into a severe ponytail at the back of her head, but her eyes were bloodshot and he wondered if her long sleeves covered needle tracks. Her hands were trembling. And her presence here, in his home, was a punch in the gut.

Jules was visibly uncomfortable, sitting on the edge of a club chair made for relaxing, and he wondered why she hadn't called him. Unless maybe he had it backward. Maybe Jules had set the visit up after their conversation last night.

The flash of anger was gone as quickly as it came. Jules was incredibly protective. There was no way she would willingly allow Vicky anywhere near the girls, not until custody was settled, and maybe not even then. And their own relationship might be far from what appearances suggested, but he knew she'd protect him, too. He frowned. "What are you doing here, Vicky?"

She flinched slightly at his tone, but recovered quickly, smoothing her face into an ingratiating smile. "I heard my firstborn was in town and I wanted to see you, Cameron. It's been too long. You look wonderful. And I wanted to see the girls, too, of course."

"That's not happening."

Jules's eyes snapped to his and she looked worried, so he crossed to her and sat on the arm of the chair, resting his hand on her shoulder.

It was hard for him to think of Vicky as his mother, because as far as he was concerned, the person who'd mothered him ceased to exist after she'd turned her back on him. "You filed a petition for custody, Vicky. You shouldn't even be here."

"Jules isn't texting me back," she said, a petulant tone to her voice. "They're *my* grandchildren."

He sucked in a deep breath, fearing that he was going to say something he would regret, something she could use against them in court. Jules groped for his hand, then gripped his fingers.

Vicky turned narrowed eyes toward the two of them, a sneer forming on her face as she changed tactics. "I bet you two are having a fine time spending the money the girls inherited from Glory on this big fancy house. I hate to do it, but I'm gonna have to tell the judge about it—for the girls' own good."

"You go ahead and tell the judge whatever you want," Cam laughed, even though the accusation wasn't funny. He should've known this little family reunion was all about the money. In fact, he and Jules had figured that from the beginning. They just hadn't realized how bold Vicky was, or maybe how desperate.

Jules cleared her throat. "Mrs. Porter, Cam's a very successful author. He doesn't need Eleanor and Emma's money."

Of course, Vicky turned on her, then, too, stammering and indignant. "It doesn't matter what kind of stunts you pull—you're not going to get to keep them. You're not even related to them. I'm their grandmother and the judge is going to give me custody. Glory shoulda put that in the will, anyway."

"I think Glory had a good idea of what was best for the girls." Cam stood and took a couple of deliberate steps toward the door. "It's time for you to go now."

Vicky shook her head and sat back down on the couch. "Not until I see the girls."

Pulling his phone out of his pocket, he handed it to Jules. "Call your brother. Tell him we need a patrol car out here. There's someone trespassing on our property."

Vicky's eyes went wide. "Stop—I'll leave, but I'm going to tell the judge you wouldn't let me see my own flesh and blood."

"You're not getting custody of them. If I have to fight you until every last cent of my money is gone, and I have to work until I'm 110, I will not give up fighting you on this. Eleanor and Emma deserve parents who care about them and love them, parents who put them first. They deserve *parents*."

Vicky stood in the open door, anger making her face blotchy. Ah, there she was, the woman who'd watched as his entire life was torn from him. It shouldn't surprise him, but her next words shook him, anyway. "I should've let Jerry kill you when he wanted to. At least then you would've stayed gone."

He heard Juliet's gasp from behind him. He waited until his mother had gotten into her car and turned onto the highway before he faced Jules with a sigh. "I might not have mentioned that my stepdad was holding a gun on me when he told me I had to leave."

Jules put her arms around him. "We're not a couple. I know that. I just... I need to hug you."

He closed the circle of his arms and held her. "I'm not going to let her hurt you or the girls, Jules. You have my word."

"I know." She looked up at him, her blue eyes wide and clear. "I probably shouldn't say this, but getting kicked out of that house was probably the best thing that could've happened to you. I mean, look at you. Look what you've made with your life. And that was all you."

He couldn't help it; he kissed her forehead, stepping back with his hands in the air when Jules snapped a look at him. "I know, I know, no kissing. But come on, that doesn't count."

She studied his face and he wondered if maybe he had a telltale piece of biscuit stuck somewhere.

"Are you okay, Cam? Really okay?"

"Surprisingly, yes." He started toward the front door, picking up his keys from the table in the entrance hall. "I have a confession to make."

"Another one?" She looked wary, and honestly, after all his confessions in the last twenty-four hours, he didn't blame her.

He grinned at her. "I ate one of your biscuits, and it was amazing. Is that going on the new menu?"

"Most likely." Her shoulders relaxed and she

smiled, a genuine smile, and something eased in him, as well. "I'm thinking thick slices of ham, lettuce, tomato, maybe avocado. The sweet potato flavor is subtle, though, so maybe maple turkey would complement it better. What do you think?"

"I think we should taste-test both of them, just to be sure. I'm going to pick the girls up at day care. I want to get there a little early so I can make sure the preschool staff never lets them leave with anyone but you or me."

"I told them that already."

"It won't hurt to repeat it." As he walked to his car, he took note of his surroundings. He didn't think his mother would attempt something as heinous as trying to kidnap the girls, but honestly, he wouldn't put it past her.

While Cam went to pick up Emma and Eleanor, Jules took the opportunity to check on the progress at the construction site. April and Lanna had everything running like a top at the bakery, so she felt great about that. But when she passed the construction dumpster in the alley—booths and tables and pieces of Sheetrock piled high—she had a moment of panic. She wanted to tell the construction crew she'd changed her mind, to put it all back. Which, of course, was ridiculous.

She liked everything to be perfect and she wasn't comfortable with a mess, even if she knew logically the mess was the way through to something better. And come to think of it, that sounded like a great metaphor for her life these days, and might be the reason she'd been so unsettled about her relationship with Cameron.

It was all so complicated and messy. Very, very messy.

She pulled open the back door of the café and stepped into organized chaos. The whole place had been gutted. Dust hung in the air—a thick, choking fog. Near the front, a worker was using some kind of very loud, ear-shattering tool to remove the old vinyl tile from the concrete slab.

Colin, the contractor Latham had recommended, spotted her and walked over, shouting so he could be heard over the noise. "Mrs. Quinn. I didn't know you were going to be stopping by today, but as you can see, we're making progress. Once we demo the bakery, we'll start installing the floor in the full space. The tile got delivered. You want to check it and make sure it's the right one before we start laying it in?"

"Sure." Her head was spinning. So much was riding on just her gut and instinct. But what if she was wrong? What if her gut feeling stank?

In the corner, Colin pulled a box cutter out of his back pocket and sliced into one carton, pulling out a tile. "Now, you'll know this is tile when you see it on the floor, but the overall feel you'll get when you look at the room as a whole is warmer, like wood. And it's a lot more durable and less finicky than wood."

"It looks good. I like it!" The machine the other worker was using abruptly stopped, leaving Jules shouting into a suddenly quiet room. She cleared her throat and lowered her voice. "Yeah, it looks good. I like the exposed brick on the back wall, too."

"Glad to hear it. We've still got some structural

work to do in here, like making that back door into French doors that lead out to a courtyard, like you wanted. And we've got to replace the windows and all that, but by Monday, we'll be ready to start demo in the bakery. My crew is the best around. By the end of next week, you'll be picking out paint colors."

"Monday. Wow. Okay, I'll tell my staff, and over the weekend, we'll get it cleared out and ready for you to start work. Thanks."

"No problem. You've got my cell if you have any questions."

Jules got in her van with a million questions circling in her mind like sharks ready to feed. Would people come to the restaurant? Would they like a different menu? Was she crazy to change a formula that had worked for her mom for over twenty years?

The overwhelming urge to call her mother surfaced again. She wanted to hear her mom tell her to trust herself. She definitely didn't want to disturb the honeymooners. And what if Bertie was horrified that she was changing things? Maybe she'd just snap some pictures and email them to her. She was almost certain Bertie would be supportive, unlike Cam's mother. The two of them couldn't be more different.

So yeah, Jules had lots of questions. She just wasn't sure the contractor could answer any of them.

Cam's car was in the driveway when she pulled in. She picked up a stray sippy cup from the front steps that had probably fallen out of Eleanor's backpack. The stress she'd felt leaving the café melted away the instant she heard the giggles of two little girls.

She followed the sound of their play through the living room, down the hall and to the playroom. She had to laugh when she found Cam sitting on the floor, playing dollhouse with Eleanor.

"No, no, Uncle Cam, you say, 'I think it's time to do hair, Princess Piglet.'"

"I think it's time to do hair, Princess Piglet." He was using a falsetto voice, and as he spoke, he wiggled the pig figurine he was holding. Emma was creeping around him, her little hand fisted in his shirt for balance, and the dog was asleep, resting her head on Cam's foot.

Jules thought her heart might explode. It was one thing to put the brakes on romance when she knew for a fact he wasn't feeling the same way. It was another thing altogether to actually resist a man who cared enough about his little girls to play dollhouse.

She knew better than to fall in love with Cam. She *knew* better. But every day, she seemed to get a little bit closer. Not that she would tell him that, or could tell him that. She'd proposed a marriage of convenience, he'd agreed to it and she had to live with it, no matter how hard it was.

However, it would be super helpful if he'd stop being so incredible. If he were a jerk, it would be so much easier for Jules to remember she wasn't supposed to fall for him.

Emma looked over, saw her at the door and squealed. She let go of Cam, steadied herself and took two steps. She teetered toward Jules, looking up with a toothy, drooly grin before losing her balance.

"Oh, my goodness, Emma, not yet! Cam, did you see that? Emma took two steps!"

"No way!"

Jules dropped to the floor beside them and dug her

phone out of her back pocket. "Let's see if she can do it again so we can get it on video."

She lifted Emma to her feet and held her until she was steady. And then, as Jules held her phone in trembling hands, their tiny girl took three straight-legged steps toward Cam, arms outstretched, wobbling as she tried to balance.

"You can do it…" Cam coaxed, as she paused and swayed. "Come on, Emma, you can do it."

When Emma dived into Cam's arms, he tossed her in the air. "Woo-hoo, you did it!"

Jules tried to speak, but the lump in her throat was too big. She choked out the words, "I'll be right back," and hurried into the hall before giving in to the tears.

Burying her face in her hands, she sobbed—for Emma, because her mom wasn't here to witness this milestone. For Eleanor because she wanted her mom to tuck her in at night. She cried for Cam because he'd missed knowing his amazing sister, and last, tears for herself, because she missed Glory so, so much.

She felt a hand touch her shoulder and she turned toward him. Cam held his arms out and she stepped into them, letting him hold her, crying until her tears were spent. Finally, she eased away from him, swiping the wet streaks from under her eyes. She sniffed and winced. "Sorry about your shirt."

"It will launder. I'm sorry, too. Really sorry you're missing your best friend."

The lump in her throat was back. She swallowed hard. "It's always there, the ache of missing her, but sometimes, like now, it's overwhelming." She pressed her fingers to her forehead, trying to soothe the aching crying-jag hangover. "I really hate to cry."

"I know." His eyes were damp as well, when he smiled down at her. "If we're like this for a couple of baby steps, what are we going to be like at her high school graduation?"

Jules sniffed again, then laughed. "The other parents are going to need a boat."

He nodded and picked up Pippi, handing the tubby puppy to Jules. "She needs to go out. Would you mind?"

Jules gratefully took the puppy, snuggling the warm ball of fur into the little nook between her neck and shoulder, letting the feel of Pippi's soft weight soothe her jagged edges.

As she walked outside, her mind was on the girls and the man who cared enough about them to play dollhouse. He was a natural with Emma and Eleanor. But by his own admission, he was good at adapting, a chameleon fitting in wherever he went.

He'd held her while she cried.

But what was real? How would she even know?

Chapter Twelve

Cam double knotted the laces on his soccer cleats. It was his first time making it out for the pickup game Jules's brothers and brothers-in-law played each week with their friends. Jules had sent him off with a big bottle of water, a bag full of fruit and a wish for luck.

He didn't need luck. He'd played real soccer in places where it was called football. It was a blood sport in many countries around the world and Cam traveled with a soccer ball, even when he was traveling light. Language barriers didn't matter when it came to playing ball. Pretty much anywhere in the world, you could drop a soccer ball on the ground and instantly have a game.

Joe clapped his hands together. "Okay, let's go, guys. We have an hour. Stop messing around trying to tie your shoelaces into pretty bows."

Cam grinned and jogged into the center of the field and stood next to Jules's brother, dancing a little on his feet. He was so ready for this.

"Okay, play."

Joe dropped back and Cam went for the ball, land-ing on his rear end as Latham bodychecked him. He rolled to his feet with a laugh. "Full-contact soccer. I see how it is."

Latham dribbled the ball toward the goal, getting ready to pass to Ash.

Cam ran the ball down, stealing it from Latham and sending it downfield to Joe in a high-arcing pass. Joe took the shot but it landed in the hands of the goalie.

"How's my sister?" Ash jogged backward, waiting for the goalie to kick to put the ball back in play.

"Truth?"

Ash shrugged. "Sure."

The ball landed at Ash's feet. Cam was faster, though, and turned the ball back the other way, dropping it right into the sweet spot where Joe slammed it in for their first goal.

Ash scowled. "You were saying?"

"She's driving me crazy." Maybe not literally crazy, because he was pretty sure if he was literally crazy, he'd be a lot less *bothered* than he was right now.

Every time he tried to concentrate on writing, he got distracted. From his desk, he could look right out the glass doors and into the kitchen windows. He could see her dancing in the kitchen in her bare feet with their pale pink toenails. He didn't even want to know how he knew her toenails were pale pink. He shook his head.

Bonkers.

Ash got the pass from Latham, dribbled it downfield and took a shot on goal and missed. He jogged back toward Cam. "Crazy, how?"

"Her toenails are pink," he blurted.

Ash grinned.

Colin dribbled the ball toward Cam, who did a little sidestepping which-way-are-you-gonna-go dance before he took the ball and sent it toward his goal again, but missed wide. The ball went out of bounds.

Because he was still thinking about Jules.

Setting up for the corner kick, Ash shoulder bumped Cam to the side. "I'm a newlywed with a little kid. I feel for ya, man."

If Ash only knew. Cam drew in a frustrated breath. "She's always in the kitchen baking stuff and singing show tunes…" Which scrambled any close-to-coherent thought.

Ash stopped running, digging his cleats into the ground and cutting back the other way to receive a chest-high pass.

Cam chased the ball as Ash tried to send it downfield, but it curved out of bounds again. He picked it up for the throw-in, hurling it to the ground at Joe's feet.

To make matters worse, Jules called him down every little while to come into the kitchen with her, where all the show tune singing was happening. How was a man supposed to get a woman out of his head when she smelled like vanilla cupcakes and cooked like that? Much less get any work done?

He'd eaten French toast and muffins and thick slabs of bacon and maple turkey on a sweet potato biscuit—the clear winner. He couldn't exercise enough to make up for all the food she'd been making him taste-test. Forty-five minutes into an hour-long game and he was sucking wind.

He bent over at the waist, gulping air.

"Water break." Joe slapped him on the back. "Been eating too much of Jules's good cooking?"

"He was complaining about her pink toenails driving him crazy." Ash grabbed his water bottle from the bench with an exaggerated eye roll.

"Aw, Cam." Joe grinned. "Real men aren't bothered by a little toenail polish."

"Speak for yourself," Latham muttered.

Joe's phone buzzed from where he'd left it on the bench. "That can't be good. Everyone knows Saturday afternoons are sacred."

He picked it up and glanced at the readout. "Well, looks like no one's gonna be sleeping at our house for a while. Claire just went to the hospital to pick up a newborn. We're getting a new foster baby."

"Congratulations, Dad." Ash grinned. "You guys single-handedly keep my practice afloat."

"Boy or girl?" Cam asked.

Joe squinted at the phone. "No idea. She didn't say. I hate to do this, guys, but I need to get back to the house. Our stash of newborn diapers is low and I have no idea what we did with the bassinet after we used it the last time."

"We'll bring dinner over. We have plenty of food." Cam rolled the ball toward himself and bounced it up to his hands before tossing it to Joe to stuff in his bag. "If you need anything else, let us know."

"You've got a huge house. Go to foster parent class and get licensed so they have someone else to call sometimes." It was a throwaway comment from Joe as he swung the heavy bag of balls and cones over his shoulder and walked off to the parking lot, but it stuck in Cam's mind.

Joe and Claire—Ash and Jordan, too—took in kids no one else wanted. Kids who needed a safe place while their parents tried to get their act together. Kids like Cam.

His life would've been so different if he'd had a family like the Sheehans. It didn't do a lot of good to look back now, but looking forward to the future, maybe he could be that family for another kid.

In the back of his mind, though, the same old refrain kept playing. The one that said, *If you stick around, they're going to find out who you really are.* Then there was the old favorite: *It'll hurt less if you do the leaving.*

He was pretty sure in this case that it was going to hurt either way.

Jules looked down into the tiny newborn's face. He was sleeping, a fragile fringe of lashes curving across his cheek. Every once in a while, his mouth curled into a lopsided, milk-drunk smile. Jules was entranced.

Jules and Cam had brought over all the leftovers from her taste-testing endeavors: ham and biscuits, homemade bread, a variety of cookies, cupcakes and desserts. The only thing they'd needed to round out a pretty decent dinner were some chips and fruit, which she'd picked up at the store on the way.

Eleanor was thrilled to have a chance to play with her cousins, and Cam had taken the opportunity to throw the football with Deke. Amelia had seized Emma as soon as they got out of the car and taken her across the yard to the swings. So Jules found herself with time on her hands and an itty-bitty love in her arms.

Claire came out through the back door with two glasses of sweet tea, handed one to Jules and settled in the swing beside her. "Want me to take baby Jack? I don't want you to miss out on your break."

"He's fine. Perfect, actually." Jules patted Jack's swaddled booty. "I remember Eleanor and Emma at this age, but I didn't spend as much time with them as I wish I had now."

She watched Cam throw the ball in a long spiral toward Deke, who caught it, spun and sprinted like he was running for the end zone. The kid had talent. She hoped he'd get to stay here long enough to play next year. "You think Deke will be here for a while?"

"I'm not sure, but I think so. He's been in a couple of other foster homes, so it seems likely. It helps to have Cam spend some time with him. Deke's had a rough go of it."

Jules didn't ask any questions—it wasn't her place, or her business. Maybe given some time to build trust, Cam could encourage Deke to see that there was a life on the other side of growing up with parents who couldn't, or wouldn't, take care of you.

A couple other boys had joined in the game. Cam was showing one of the younger boys how to grip the football with his fingers parallel to the laces. Now that she looked closer, she thought maybe it was Tyler, the one who had the meltdown last week. She smiled as he managed to throw the ball in a wobbly arc and Cam gave him an exploding fist bump.

Mentoring suited him. He was good with the boys and they clearly looked up to him. She had to wonder… Was this the real Cam? She wanted to believe it. This Cam was handsome, generous, loving. And did she say handsome?

"Does he know how you feel about him?" Claire asked quietly.

"What? I mean, of course." Jules blushed, her cheeks going hot under the weight of Claire's scrutiny.

"You had such a whirlwind wedding. It's not hard to figure out that you two got married to protect the girls."

Jules let the silence stretch for a long moment, but when it came down to it, she couldn't lie. "Cam's mother filed a petition for custody. The two of us together have a stronger case than either of us alone. Or that's the theory, anyway."

"But somewhere along the way, you developed feelings for him?"

"Not exactly subtle, huh?"

Claire shot her a skeptical look. "Not much, no. But, really, who could blame you? Look at him."

Jules laughed, startling the baby in her arms. "For real. He's so sweet with the kids and with me. But because of his childhood and being on his own when he was so young, he's learned to adapt so he can fit in anywhere. I know it's a skill that's helpful to him. I just don't know if he's unconsciously trying to mold himself to fit in with our family or if he's really that good a dad." She nodded at the boys. "Really that good a mentor."

Claire pushed the swing with her foot, letting it rock for a few beats. "That's a tough one. We've had some kids come through here who are pretty good con artists. Some don't even know that's what they're doing, it's such a part of them."

Jules nodded. "Right, exactly."

"It's a survival skill, you know? Not conscious

deception." Claire squinted at one of the kids on top of the playset in the yard. "And it's an authentic part of who they are, even if it seems like it's the opposite. I don't know if that makes any sense at all."

"It does." She'd just never looked at it that way before.

Claire stood, her hand shielding her eyes from the sun. "James Frederick. Put that rock on the ground before you break House Rule Number One."

She waited until the little boy, around seven years old, complied, before she sat down again. "Kids who come from hard places do learn to adapt. They have to in order to survive." She nodded to where Cam was on the bottom of a heap of laughing boys, wrestling his way out. "But kindness and generosity, those are character traits that don't change."

Amelia bounced up the steps with Emma in her arms. Emma caught sight of Jules, registered that she was holding another baby, and screeched in anger.

Claire laughed and took the new baby from Jules. "Looks like your break time is over. Mine, too, but I'm so glad I wasn't spending this nice afternoon in the house cooking dinner. Thank you so much."

"My pleasure. I'm sure I'll have more to bring over later in the week. I'm going to bake tonight after the girls go to bed." Jules stood and settled Emma on her hip. She searched the yard for Eleanor and found her playing in the grass with a couple of half-grown kittens. Oh, man, she'd better get over there before Cam decided they needed a cat for their growing menagerie.

As she walked into the yard, Claire's insights were running through her mind. Jules had wanted Cam to be real with her. And maybe he had been. He'd shared his past. He'd shared his desire for a family and a home. He was trying.

He had trust issues and rightfully so, but she wondered if she wasn't the one with the bigger problem here.

It was after midnight when Cam walked into the kitchen with his empty mug, puzzling out a plot point in his head. His character was stuck in Casablanca and Cam had no idea how to get him out of there. Truthfully, Casablanca was beautiful and his character just wanted to stay there with his lady. Cam didn't blame him. But this was an adventure story and adventures must be had.

He didn't even realize Jules was working in the kitchen until he was halfway into the room. She had her earphones in and was singing along with a song he recognized from a current musical on Broadway. Maybe a little off-key, but man, she was beautiful when she wasn't so careful.

She had a little smudge of flour on her cheek and was stirring something on the stove that smelled amazing. Oh, no—she wasn't stirring it, she was stuffing cupcakes with it. He stifled a groan.

"Jules."

No response.

"Jules." He tapped her on the shoulder.

She screamed and whirled around. Snatching her earbuds out of her ears, she smacked him with a dish towel. "You should know better than to sneak up on a person!"

He laughed and nipped the dish towel out of her

hand. "Don't blame me—it's not my fault you had your music turned up so loud you couldn't hear me."

Jules scowled at him and held up a spoon of some kind of sticky golden goo. "Okay, you might have a point there. Want a taste?"

"What is it?"

"You have to taste it and see. Just how brave are you?"

"Well, I've eaten tarantulas in Cambodia. I can probably handle anything you throw at me." He opened his mouth to continue his list of weird foods, but she stuffed the spoon in before he could speak.

His knees threatened to buckle. It was that good. "Jules. Seriously."

"Okay, now try it like this." She handed him a cupcake. "It's a butter cake with pecan pie filling, topped with a bourbon–brown sugar frosting."

He bit into the cupcake. The butter cake was tender, the pecan pie filling gooey and the frosting melded it all together in one delectable bite. He might die of a sugar rush, but if he did, he'd die a happy man.

She raised her eyebrows. "Well…?"

"Jules, I'm not exaggerating when I say that's probably the best thing I've ever eaten in my entire life." He went to the refrigerator and pulled out the milk.

"That's exactly the response I was going for." She sent a sparkling grin his way, turned back to the counter and piped a perfect swirl on the next cupcake.

"How do you do that?" He downed a cup of milk and swiped the back of his fist across his mouth.

"It's all in the wrist. Watch." She moved to the next cupcake and piped a swirl.

"You didn't even move your wrist."

Jules laughed. "Sure I did. Want to try it?"

He cut his eyes at her. "Of course I want to try it. Give me that thing."

She held it out to him. "Cradle it gently. Like you're holding a baby chick."

He dropped his hand. "Now you're just messing with me."

Cracking up, she tried to keep a straight face and failed. "I'm not. I'm really not."

She offered him the pastry bag again. He took it, holding it between his hands like he was about to play some tennis. She laughed again and then said, "Don't worry. You're not hopeless."

Standing slightly behind him, she reached around and closed his fingers around the top of the bag, where it was twisted shut. Her scent surrounded him, and every touch of her body against his arm was a unique kind of torture.

"This is your flow control, so to speak. How much pressure you use here affects how much frosting comes out at the tip." With her fingers still over his, she gently applied pressure and made the tiniest circle with her wrist to make the frosting swirl on the cupcake.

Cam stepped back, away from her, and looked at it critically. "Nope. I'm gonna have to eat that one. Or I would, if I wouldn't go into a sugar coma. I think I've got it. Let me try."

His lip caught firmly between his teeth in concentration, he made a large uneven swirl on top of the next cupcake. He frowned at it. "That doesn't look like yours."

"It takes a lot of practice to make them the same every time. Want to try some more?"

"No one would want to eat the ones I made." He handed the bag of frosting back to her and watched in amazement as she deftly frosted twelve cupcakes in the time he'd painstakingly frosted one.

With a final flourish, she frosted the last cupcake and laid down the bag. She lifted her finger to her lips and gently sucked the frosting from the tip.

All the blood left Cam's head. He closed his eyes. *No kissing. No kissing. No kissing.*

When he opened them again, Jules was at the sink, washing the pans, and he realized she was humming to herself again and her feet were bare, showing those blasted pink toenails.

He left his coffee cup on the counter and fled the room. She was his wife, and for some weird reason thinking about that made it easier to resist her. He liked Jules. More, he respected her. He respected the friendship that was growing between them, despite all the obstacles to it.

They'd crossed that bridge, and then they'd blown it up. There was no going back now. He was just going to have to learn to live with their decision to remain friends, no matter how distracting her pink toenails were.

Chapter Thirteen

Jules was in the bedroom trying to wrestle Eleanor into a pair of tights while Cam was in the adjoining bathroom with Emma in the bathtub. He called out to her, "I think maybe it would've been a better idea if I got dressed after I gave Emma a bath."

"She does love to splash." Jules dropped Eleanor's legs and picked up the tights' packaging. It said 4T, but there was no way these things were the right size. Finally, she managed to stuff both of Eleanor's legs into the tights, but when she got the waistband over the little girl's hips, there was still a huge gap…and a hole in the waist where Jules's thumb had poked through during the tug-of-war. "Forget it. You can wear leggings and that cute striped shirt."

"Where we going?" Eleanor asked for the thirtieth time.

"We're going to your school. It's spaghetti supper night." Another reason to go with leggings and a tunic rather than the dress she'd planned. Maybe El wouldn't be as dressed up as some of the kids, but at least Jules wouldn't be freaking out about how to get spaghetti stains out of a dressy dress.

"Why?"

"Because all your friends will be there. You're going to sing, remember?"

"Miss Marla said we're gonna sing for the mamas and daddies." Eleanor bounced on the bed as Jules pulled the tunic over her head.

Jules imagined herself dropping a truth bomb on Eleanor's teacher. Surely, Eleanor wasn't the only kid without a mom who went to that preschool. In fact, Jules knew she wasn't. A lot of Claire and Joe's foster kids had gone to that school.

"There will be lots of other people besides mamas and daddies. There will be grandmas and grandpas and aunts and uncles and brothers and sisters, like Emma. And all the teachers and friends. It will be so much fun. I can't wait to hear you sing."

"Alice has a new baby brother and she said in circle time that da baby was in her mama's tummy."

Oh, good gravy, where was she going with this? Jules sent up a quick prayer for patience as she tugged on Eleanor's bright purple leggings. "Uh-huh…"

"I was in your tummy, right?"

Jules went still. It had been a month or so since Eleanor had mentioned Glory being in heaven with Jesus, but Jules had no idea she was so confused. "No, honey. You grew in your mama Glory's tummy."

The three-year-old scrunched her little nose up. "But babies grow in da *mama's* tummy."

Time to change tactics. Jules pulled a pair of lace-edged socks off the pile of clean clothes and slid them onto Eleanor's feet. "Did you see me holding that little baby at the farm on Saturday?"

Eleanor nodded. "His wittle ears were so cute."

"I knew you when you were just that little. I got to hold you when you weren't even an hour old. Did you know that? Oh, you were so cute. I knew you were going to be special."

Eleanor nodded. Hearing that she was special was nothing new for her. "But you're my mom, right? I can call you Mama?"

After weeks of Jules skirting the black hole in her mind, Eleanor went and pushed her in. She felt like she was cartwheeling through darkness and there were no handholds to grab onto in order to slow her flight. She sat down on the bed beside Eleanor and took a deep breath. She might be in the darkness, but she had to be the handholds for Eleanor. "You can call me whatever you want, El. You can call me Aunt Jules or Lili or Mom or even Silly Alligator."

Eleanor giggled. "I think I want to call you Mama. But what about Uncle Cam?"

Jules picked Eleanor up, set her on her feet and straightened her dress. "I think you should call him Boo-boo Head."

Eleanor giggled. "Or I could call him Daddy. And then I'd have a mama and daddy to sing to at the pasketti supper at school. Can I have a snack now?"

"Sure you can. There are some oatmeal cookies on the kitchen table."

Jules gathered the clothes that were scattered on the bed and sat for a minute, holding them all in her hands.

Cam came out of the bathroom with Emma wrapped

in a yellow towel with a duck-shaped hood. "You handled that great. You made her happy and she feels secure."

Tears gathered in Jules's eyes. "I feel like I'm cheapening the memory of Glory being Eleanor's mom. I don't want to be her replacement."

"When Eleanor gets a little older and she understands, you can tell her stories. It'll mean a lot to her that you'll keep her mom alive in her memory. But for now, she just wants a mama and a daddy like everyone else."

"I guess you're right," Jules said slowly. "I'll get Emma dressed if you want to go change your shirt."

He handed Emma over and started for the door. "Won't take me but a minute and then I'll put Eleanor in the car. Meet you out front?"

"Sure thing, Boo-boo Head." She grinned as she heard his response drift back from the hall.

"Very funny, Silly Alligator."

She laid Emma on the changing table and slid a diaper underneath her, still thinking about Cam and how they seemed to be building a rapport. Their relationship wasn't nearly as guarded, although they had an unspoken agreement to avoid physical contact when they were alone.

Well, since last Saturday at least, when she'd shown him how to frost cupcakes. She'd come so close to reaching up to pull him down for a kiss. Instead she'd busied herself with the dishes. Plunging her hands in ice-cold water hadn't helped much, but when she'd turned around, he'd been gone.

With her hand on Emma's tummy to keep her from rolling off the table, she reached into the drawer and pulled out the matching dress to Eleanor's. Emma screeched when Jules pulled it over her head, but Jules handed her a toy and she was soon happily chewing on it.

Jules's phone buzzed in her back pocket. Somehow she'd missed a call or it had gone straight to voice mail. She tapped the entry and a voice she didn't know began to speak.

"This call is for Juliet Quinn. My name is Patience Carter. I'm the attorney assigned to be the guardian ad litem for Eleanor and Emma Prentiss. I'd like to drop by in the morning for a quick visit, if that's convenient for you. I have an hour between 8:00 a.m. and 9:00 a.m., so unless I hear from you, I'll see you then."

She pulled little lacy socks onto Emma's feet and lifted the baby into her arms. *Eight o'clock? Tomorrow morning?*

That was fifteen hours from now. This room was a mess. The whole house was a mess. Jules had been cooking and baking for days straight and there were toys and clothes and dog bones spread all over the house. Hopefully, the GAL would understand.

Oh, Lord, please help.

There was so much riding on this.

Cam's first thought when he opened the door for the guardian ad litem was that they were in so much trouble. She had a huge bag, and was wearing a skirt suit and tennis shoes.

Practical *and* proper. Awesome.

"I'm Cameron Quinn. Please, come in."

"Patience Carter, the guardian ad litem. What a lovely home."

"Thank you. We like it."

Jules came out of the kitchen with a plate of cookies and a suddenly shy three-year-old. "I'm Juliet. It's nice to meet you. This is Eleanor."

Patience immediately got down on Eleanor's level and held out her hand. "It's very nice to meet you."

Eleanor hid her face in Jules's pant leg, but held her hand out for the lady to shake.

"Emma's napping right now. She's trying to give up the morning nap but we're hanging on for dear life." Jules was babbling, the plate trembling so hard in her hands that Cam was afraid the cookies were going to slide right off. He took the plate and slid it onto the coffee table. Eleanor immediately helped herself, shyness disappearing.

"Do you like cookies, Eleanor?" Patience asked.

El nodded enthusiastically. "With choc'ate chips."

"How about dolphins?" The GAL dug in her huge bag and came out with a small stuffed toy. "I brought this for you. My daughter is a marine biologist and she works with dolphins. She's very smart, just like you."

"Mama says smart is better than pretty." Eleanor took the toy with a polite thank-you and climbed into Cam's lap, while he tried not to laugh.

Jules buried her head in her hand before looking up at Patience with a wince. "It's true. I did say that."

"She calls you Mama?" Patience wrote something on her notepad.

"Yes, it's kind of new." She sent a help-me look to Cam.

"There was a program at the preschool last night and all the parents were there to watch. Eleanor sang with her class. She was a star." He gave his niece a little tickle and she fell back, laughing.

"That's great, Eleanor." To Cam and Jules, she said, "But she's putting you two in that role, so that's interesting. Are there paternal grandparents?"

Jules answered this one. "Yes, Sam's parents are living, but they have a home in a retirement community in Florida—one that doesn't allow children. They're planning a visit this summer, though."

"You two are newlyweds?" She looked at Cam for this question.

He nodded, with a smile for Jules. "We are."

Eleanor slid off his lap, pulled out a basket of blocks from under the coffee table and dumped them to the floor with a clatter.

"And do you mind me asking how you fell in love so quickly?" Patience went still, waiting for the answer, her pencil poised over her notepad, and Cam thought, *This is the heart of her questions. She wants to know our motivation.*

He sat back in his chair with an indulgent smile for Jules. "The last time I saw Juliet, she was a skinny six-year-old with braids and freckles, playing with my sister. You can imagine how shocked I was to see this *beautiful* woman walk into the room… But it was the way she tended to my nieces that really drew me. She's got such a huge heart and she puts it on the line with everything she does. I know it seems crazy, but I don't how I could've resisted."

Cam let the moment stretch as Jules's eyes widened, her smile trembling. He turned to Patience. "Of course, we got married so quickly so that my nieces would have a stable situation with two loving parents."

"Right. Juliet, anything to add?"

She smiled at him. "Cam is accomplished and brilliant, which I admire. But the thing I love the most about him is that he's kind and he cares about people. The girls and I are very lucky to have him in our lives."

The attorney made another note on her pad as Cam tried to breathe. Jules almost sounded like a person who really knew him, really cared about him. He'd said things, too, about how beautiful she was and how he couldn't resist her. And the funny thing was, he'd meant every word. Was it possible Jules had real feelings for him?

No. Their relationship was pretend. Getting caught up in the what-ifs was a no-win prospect. He needed to put it out of his mind and focus on what he could influence. He needed to remember who he was.

The sound of Emma waking up with mumbles and whines filtered through to them from the baby monitor on the kitchen counter.

Patience looked up with a smile. "Oh, good, it sounds like our other little girl is waking up. Do you mind if I follow you back, so I can see the living arrangements?"

Jules jumped to her feet, smoothing her clothes. "Not at all."

"I'll start warming Emma's bottle." Cam cut across the room toward the kitchen, pausing to touch Jules's elbow and say quietly, "You're doing great. Hang in there. We're almost done."

If they could just make it through the next few minutes with no disasters, they'd be home free.

"It's just back this way. There's a Jack and Jill bath between the two rooms, but we've made the adjoining bedroom into a playroom so they could stay together. They shared a room before." Jules led the way down the hall. Emma's vocalizations were getting increasingly grumpier the longer it took them to reach her room.

She opened the door a crack and Emma let out a squeal of glee, her hands already reaching for Jules. She laughed and plucked Emma out of the crib. "Hi, baby girl!"

"What a precious baby. Hi, Emma!"

Emma hid her face in Jules's shoulder. "She's almost always happy. We had a rough week when she was teething and had an ear infection, but other than that, she's an easy baby."

"That's great. You're doing a wonderful job with them, Jules. It can't have been easy, but I can tell they're attached to you and to Cam, and that's important."

"I've been a part of their lives since they were born. I—I don't know how much to say, but Glory and I were friends since preschool and there's a reason she wanted the girls to be with me if something happened to her."

"I'll consider that, but my job is to do my own investigation and make a recommendation to the court based only on what I believe is best for the girls. I know it's hard to trust someone you've never met before, but I've been doing this a long time. I know what I'm doing."

"I understand." She followed Patience out of the girls' room and back to the living area. What she really wanted to do was find a corner and have a quiet cry. These past few months it had taken everything Jules had to survive, and every time she felt like she was coming out on the other side, something else popped up.

In the living room, Cam handed her a bottle, which Emma grabbed and voraciously attacked.

Patience cleared her throat and pointed toward the coffee table, where Eleanor was seated, happily feeding oatmeal cookies to a humongous black puppy.

"Oh, no." Cam's eyes widened. "Pippi, get down!"

Pippi hung her big head, her ears drooping, but she obeyed. And promptly threw up on the carpet.

The three of them—Jules, Cam and the GAL—all stood in silence for a long few seconds, their mouths hanging open.

The guardian ad litem started laughing. "I think I'm gonna go now. It was so nice meeting you all."

She left through the front door, still giggling.

Cam closed the door and turned to look at Jules. "That went well, I think."

Jules wasn't sure whether to laugh or cry, but the laugh bubbled up before she could decide.

A little hysterical, maybe, but oh, well. "If Patience was hoping to get a real look at the inner workings of our little family, she certainly got what she wanted."

Cam wiped tears of laughter from his eyes. "Boy, did she."

"Aunt Ju—I mean, Mama, you wanna cookie?"

Jules started to laugh again. "Did the dog lick that one?"

Eleanor looked at it. "Uh-huh."

"No, thank you. I think I'll wait." Jules dropped into a chair with Emma in her lap, still giggling. "And maybe you should pick another one."

Cam shooed the dog out the back door. "I think we're going to have to get a new carpet."

Emma reached up, rubbing a piece of Jules's hair between her fingers, like she always did when she was taking a bottle or getting sleepy. And suddenly, Jules wanted to cry again, but she didn't. Instead, she prayed.

God, please. Please protect these babies.

Jules had experienced tragedy. Her big brother Ash had gone through cancer and the treatment left him a diabetic. Her dad had died of a heart attack way too young. Her best friend had died in a car accident.

But nothing… *Nothing* had put her on her face on the ground, begging God for His mercy and protection. Not like this. The future of those sweet girls, and their future as a family, was in the hands of a judge who'd never met any of them.

And she was absolutely powerless.

But God wasn't.

Chapter Fourteen

"And then, just as we were about to be home free, we walked into the living room and the dog was standing on the coffee table—with Eleanor—wolfing down the cookies." Cam unlocked the front door to the Hilltop, his travel coffee mug in hand.

Latham's deep laugh rolled out. "When our first guardian ad litem visited, Levi was potty training and he dropped his pants right in the front yard as we were waving goodbye to her." Latham paused. "Jordan didn't think it was nearly as funny as I did."

"I had no idea what adventures were waiting for me in Red Hill Springs." Cam laughed in turn as he walked to the bank of light switches and flipped them on one by one. Gone were the fluorescent panel lights. In their place were recessed lights and huge orb-like light fixtures that somehow managed to look simultaneously homey and chic.

A few more Saturdays and this place would be ready to open. Then what would Cam do?

Finish his book. That would make his publisher happy. But then what?

Normally when Cam finished one project, he couldn't wait to get on the road again. A new wild adventure, a brand-new story to write: his own *and* his characters'. His tradition for finishing a book was a steak dinner and a dive into his files, letting his imagination begin to work on the next one. It was his favorite thing about his life—the challenge and the novelty of constant change.

So why wasn't he excited?

Latham took a slow turn, taking it all in. "They're really making progress in here. Even with an expanded kitchen in the bakery, it looks huge. And with those new windows, it looks light and spacious. I love the exposed brick. It's gonna be gorgeous."

"The counter and bakery case are going in this week. Jules has to pick out the tables and Wynn's coming in to paint some words or something on the walls. I wasn't consulted on that decision."

"Any problems with construction?" Latham asked.

"Some of the electricity wasn't up to code, and since we were expanding we had to work on that, but that's been the only really big thing. There was some dry rot in the bathroom wall, but we kind of figured that. There's nothing much left now of the original place."

"What does Bertie think?"

"Jules emailed her a few pictures when it was all gutted. To be honest, I don't think they've talked about it too much. When Bertie decided to let go, she left everything in Jules's hands."

Cam opened the French doors that led to a decked courtyard with a portico and an outdoor fireplace. "The string lights will go up this week, too."

Latham sat down on one of the benches that had already been installed and stretched his legs out, admiring the space. "This was such a great idea. The Hilltop will be a gathering spot, not just a diner."

"That was kind of the plan. I'm glad you like it. Jules said you helped her with the reclaimed pieces in the bakery, so if you have anything you think might work in here, let me know."

"I will. I know I have some big pieces of lumber that would make great open shelves. I'll send a picture over to Jules when I get back to the shop this afternoon." Latham took out his phone and typed a reminder to himself.

"I'll let her know." Cam took a swig of his coffee.

"I've read a couple of your books. Guardian ad litem visits notwithstanding, Red Hill Springs is not exactly an adventure travel destination."

"Trust me, being married is adventure enough."

Latham snorted a laugh. "Have to agree there. Especially when you're married to a hardheaded Sheehan woman."

"Without a doubt. Though I like to think of it as grit."

"*Grit*'s a good word for it," Latham laughed. "I wouldn't put money on anyone else in a fight and I know y'all have got one with the custody stuff going on."

"Yeah, we'll both feel a lot better when that's all sorted out." And when it was, Jules wouldn't need him anymore. And there was the problem he hadn't foreseen when he made the deal.

It wasn't supposed to hurt when he went back to

traveling. He would see them, he guessed, if he came home to write, but it wouldn't be the same.

"I know how that is. Once we adopted Penny, we petitioned for custody of her little brother, who's also in foster care. So far, even though it's been over a year, the judge is still letting it drag out. It's frustrating and hard, especially when you think you know what's best for the kids."

"It really is." Cam looked at his watch. "It's time for me to go. I promised Jules I'd keep the kids so she could go out to the farm. I think they're redecorating the cottage or something."

"Yeah, I said I'd install a baby gate at the bottom of the stairs to the loft. It's a surprise, but they're redoing it for Kiera. She's a success story like... Well, like you. She landed at Red Hill Farm as one of the first foster kids, seventeen and with a brand-new baby, but she graduated from high school and started college. She's in nursing school now."

"That's... Wow." Cam admired that kind of tenacity. It was flattering that Latham compared her to him, but he wasn't sure he deserved it.

He'd thought the past couldn't touch him anymore, but that was before he came back to Red Hill Springs. He might look like a success on the outside, but on the inside he was still the same kid no one wanted.

Jules dragged the couch to the spot under the window. "What if we put the couch here? We can use the round coffee table and put the new white chairs on the other side?"

Wynn stepped back. "I don't know. I like the idea

of Kiera being able to sit on the couch with her feet up and watch TV."

Claire stepped back in turn and looked at the room critically. "Oh, what if we leave it arranged like this, but instead of putting the TV above the mantel, we put it on that wall across from the sofa? That way, it's at a better angle for a three-year-old, too."

"Spoken like a true mom," Jordan said, from one of the stools at the kitchen island. At thirty-seven weeks pregnant, she'd been banned from moving furniture. She didn't look up from her texting. "I think I might have something that will work as a TV table in the attic. Claire's attic, I mean."

"What if you get rid of that blue velvet couch altogether? That thing is an eyesore." Latham screwed in the last anchor for the baby gate and stepped back to make sure it closed.

"No" came the simultaneous response from the women. Jules laughed.

"It's tradition," Wynn said. "The blue couch stays. Okay, so let's think about this. When Joe had the cabin, it was decorated by a twelve-year-old. When Jordan moved in, she was too busy to redecorate, so the vibe was shabby chic."

Jordan looked up from her phone. "Ouch. At least I painted over Joe's awful paint job."

"Very true. Sorry." Wynn gestured to the stairs. "I added the loft and went with farmhouse industrial, which is when the walls were painted white. I think the walls can stay white, but what's going to be the vibe for Kiera?"

Claire dropped into one of the new chairs. "She works so hard. I think we should make her home kind of funky and fun. So let's use the rug with the multi-colored geometric pattern."

"Perfect." Jules dragged the rug with the bright design into the center of the room and unrolled it. "I love it with the blue couch."

The door opened and Joe came in with a library table. "I believe the pregnant lady requested this?"

Claire pointed to the blank space on the wall opposite the couch. "Right there." She stepped back to take a look as Joe muscled it into place. "Perfect. Thanks, honey."

"Anytime, babe." He tugged her to him and kissed her nose. "Mrs. Matthews just got here to keep the kids, so I'm gonna play some basketball. Latham, you coming?"

Latham didn't even look at Wynn, just packed up his tools and followed Joe to the door, where they were both intercepted by Claire. "Basketball first, but then I need you to bring Kiera's bed down from the main house, along with Kendra's toddler bed."

Jules smothered a smile as she flipped through some large unframed canvases that Wynn had brought down from her loft studio. She turned one around. "Wynn, what's this?"

Her sister, wearing denim overalls rolled up to her ankles and paint-splattered tennis shoes, walked closer. "Oh, I did that with the kids one afternoon. I sketched in the tree and they made the leaves with their hands, which explains all the crazy colors."

"Can we put this one over the fireplace?"

"Absolutely." Wynn picked it up and placed it on the mantel, then added a plant on one side and some chunky candlesticks on the other.

With the furniture in place and the mantel looking

like it belonged in a real home, Claire turned to Wynn. "You think there's still any ice cream in that freezer?"

"It's kind of a necessity, so yeah. I'm pretty sure I put some in there last week when I was upstairs packing up the studio."

Jordan pulled the half-gallon container of rocky road out of the freezer and set it on the counter with a *clunk*. Four spoons from the drawer followed.

"We probably have an hour before Joe gets back down here with the beds." Claire pried off the lid. "So let's go over the rules. What we talk about in ice-cream time stays between us. We spill our secrets and then we feel better."

Jordan nodded. "Right. So, Jules…"

"What?" Jules looked up from the tub of ice cream, her full spoon in her hand, and squeaked, *"Me?"*

"Yeah. It's your turn." Jordan gazed directly into her eyes. "Gotta ask the big question first—have you told Cam you're in love with him?"

"Claire!" Jules shot a look at her sister-in-law who'd clearly spilled the beans.

Claire held up her hands. "I didn't say a word. I didn't have to, Jules. Everyone can see how you look at him, but…we can also see you're not happy with the way things are."

"So what's the problem?" Jordan took a huge bite of ice cream and talked around it. "You got married for the girls, I assume."

Jules shook her head. This afternoon was not turning out the way she'd anticipated. "I don't want to talk about this."

Wynn stuck her spoon into the tub of rocky road.

"None of us had an easy road to love. If we had, we wouldn't be eating ice cream all the time."

Jules looked from one woman to the next, searching for—what—maybe an out? She put her spoon down and buried her face in her hands. She could almost feel their stares.

But the truth was, she didn't need an out, she needed them. Trying to keep everything to herself was terrible. And it wasn't working.

She lifted her head. "I freaked out when I heard Glory and Cam's mom filed for custody of the girls. The judge supposedly favors biological family and two-parent families, and I figured if I could get Cam to marry me, it would kill two birds with one stone. Essentially, I got married to change my demographic."

Jordan put her spoon down and it clanged on the granite countertop. "A marriage of convenience?"

"You could call it that, except it's been pretty much anything but convenient. Especially not the part where I fell in love with—" She stopped midsentence.

Maybe her feelings weren't real; maybe it was just the situation. She normally didn't rush into decisions. There was just so much emotion inherent in this whole thing they were doing.

Because if it was true that she was in love with Cam, she had no idea what to do.

"If you're in love with him, what's the problem?" Jordan, her mouth full again, gestured with her spoon.

Jules scratched her forehead. How did she even put this into words? "We have this perfect life on the outside. He's gorgeous and smart—"

"And rich," Wynn interjected.

Jules shot her sister a look. "He's made a successful

life. But he had such an awful childhood. I think he feels like he's not capable of love or worthy of it, maybe? I think that's why he travels all the time. About the time he has to trust someone, he leaves."

"Oh, Jules." Claire covered Jules's hand with hers. "Do you think he's going to leave you and the girls?"

"I don't know." Jules's eyes filled with tears and she fought to get the words out. "He wants a family. He wants to stay in town. I know that. His mother just…really broke something inside him."

"You have to tell him how you feel." Wynn straightened.

"No…"

"No, she's right, Jules. If you love him, you have to tell him." Jordan dug her spoon into the ice cream again. "He needs it."

"He's not a project. I can't *fix* him." And what if he rejected her? Because that was Jules's biggest fear. That she'd tell him she loved him and he would leave.

"Jules, there's something you need to know. Love stinks." Jordan said it matter-of-factly.

Wynn nearly spit out her ice cream as she burst out laughing. "This is encouraging?"

"It's not all roses and unicorns, Wynn," Jordan continued. "But it's worth it." She turned back to Jules. "You've got to lay it out there so that he knows you aren't like his mom. You aren't like other people who failed him. You can't fix him, but you can love him. It's the only way you have a chance—the only way he has a chance."

"It's just so complicated." At Jordan's huffy sigh, Jules relented. "I'll think about it, okay?" She took another bite of ice cream. "I thought this ritual was supposed to make you feel better. I feel awful."

She laid her spoon on the counter and sat back, barely listening as the conversation went on around her. She wanted Cam to know she loved him, but after their last relationship talk, she was so scared.

If she told him, it would mean leaping without first knowing what was going to happen, which was something she did not *ever* do. She was a planner, a perfectionist. This was well established. Telling Cameron she loved him would be the biggest jump she'd ever taken.

A jump without a safety net.

Chapter Fifteen

Cam tiptoed out of the girls' bedroom. They were finally—*finally*—both asleep. Eleanor had pulled out every trick in the book, from needing water to wanting him to witness her newly acquired flipping trick to needing to go to the bathroom...three times.

He snagged the baby monitor off the counter in the kitchen and went in search of Jules. He could see her silhouette as she sat in one of the Adirondack chairs on the back deck beside the fire pit, the fire sending sparks like fireflies into the sky. As he got closer, he couldn't help it—he had to skim a hand over the silky sheen of her blond hair. "Hi."

Jules looked up at him. "I was hoping you'd join me."

"Eleanor decided to make Custer's last stand. It was a hard-fought battle, but alas, she was overcome." He poked the fire and added another log before dropping into the chair beside her. "What are you thinking about out here alone in the dark?"

She stayed silent for a long few seconds, a variety of emotions flickering across her face with the firelight, then took a deep breath and said, "Did you know that I'm extremely opposed to taking risks?"

He gave her a quizzical look. "May I remind you that we eloped barely thirty-six hours after having met as adults?"

She laughed. "That would seem to disprove my point, but no."

Cam tried again. "What about the Hilltop? Aren't you taking a huge risk reimagining the café?"

She tilted her head to the side, narrowing her eyes. "You'd think. But the truth is I wouldn't have had the courage to do that without you."

He glanced at her in surprise. "Jules, I just helped you figure out what you wanted to do."

"Exactly." She looked down, picking at the seams of the quilt she had wrapped around her. "Also, I've always been the peacemaker in the family. I don't like when people don't get along. Like, I bet you didn't know that I despise the name Jules."

"What? Now I know you're exaggerating."

"Abhor it. I only like Juliet marginally better."

He sat in silence for a minute, staring into the fire. "So that's why Eleanor was calling you Aunt Lili?"

"Glory was the only person I told how much I hated my name. She hated hers, too, back then. When we were eleven or twelve, we made a list of about forty options for each of us, but *Lili* was the only one for me that stuck. Eleanor adopted the nickname as an infant."

"I'm stunned."

Jules flashed him a grin. "It's shocking. I know. But even baking… I love it, don't get me wrong…

but there's nothing edgy about it. Cake makes people happy."

"Huh." This wasn't the conversation he was expecting to have tonight. He studied Jules's—Juliet's—face.

She turned toward him then. "I say all that so that when I say this next thing, you'll know it's not something that comes easily to me."

Cam felt a frisson of fear. This was the moment he'd been praying would never come, the moment when she told him that when the girls were safe, their sham of a marriage would be over. That she would have to move on with her life with the girls.

Without him.

She swallowed hard and he wanted to stop her before she started. He clenched his fist to keep from reaching out to her, to beg her not to say it. To give him another chance. He could do better, be better.

But instead, he waited, his eyes on hers.

"Jules—Juliet, whatever you want to say, it can't be that bad."

"It's not. I thought it might be bad, but I was wrong. I mean, it's not all roses and unicorns obviously…" She paused and looked down, a small, secret smile on her face, and he thought, *She's so beautiful and she doesn't even know it.*

She turned her gaze on him and he could see the reflection of the firelight in her eyes. "It's just… I love you."

His jaw dropped. Of all the things he'd expected to hear come out of her mouth, that wasn't even in the top five. "What did you say?"

"I said I love you. I didn't want to. It would be so

much simpler if we just had an arrangement." She lifted one shoulder in a slight shrug. "But, Cam, I've never met anyone like you."

He blew out a laugh and looked up, to where the stars were pinpoints of light in a dark black sky. "That's probably for the best."

"No, I don't think so. I know that's how you see yourself, but it's not how I see you. You're gentle and loving with the girls, kind and generous with the kids at Red Hill Farm. Maybe you had to do some bad things to survive, but you did survive and you built yourself into this amazing, wonderful person."

"Jules, you don't know what you're talking about. I wish what you're saying was true, but it's just not."

"You're wrong," she said, and he laughed. She was unbelievable. Beautiful and perfect, his Juliet. And oh, he wanted her to be right. He wanted it so badly that he didn't know how his heart was still in his chest and not on the ground at her feet.

Tears formed in her eyes. "We have a family. Two amazing, precious daughters who are counting on us, who also love you. Do you honestly think you're the only one who's afraid of getting their guts ripped out by this?"

"Jules… I—" He stopped when she put her hand on his.

"There's that old saying, that the real you is the person you are when no one else is watching. I know who you are when no one else is watching. I love the person who plays dollhouse with a three-year-old and walks the floor with a teething baby. Who taste-tests four hundred different cupcake flavors and—" her breath hitched "—who creates a first dance for the bride who didn't get one. I love *you*.

"You don't have to say anything—I don't even want you to say anything. I just wanted you to know." She stood up, dropping the quilt in the chair and wrapping her arms around her middle. "Church tomorrow. I'm gonna try to get some sleep."

She gave him a quick hug, leaning over his shoulders from behind, then took the monitor from the table beside him and left him sitting there staring into the fire. He rubbed the ache in his chest where his heart was still trying to find a beat. He wanted to believe her.

He longed to believe her.

Unlike Jules, Cam thought of himself as a risk-taker. A survivor. He'd managed not only to live after being tossed out at age fifteen, he'd thrived. But something was missing. Something had always been missing.

Cam had never told anyone else about the day he'd gotten thrown out of his family, but that was the day that everything had changed. He'd wanted so desperately for his mother to call his name, to tell him he mattered, but she didn't. The one person who should've loved him unconditionally couldn't.

Juliet would find out eventually that he wasn't the person she thought he was. And it would be so much worse than if he'd just never loved her to begin with. He'd had these few months of having a family, of feeling like he was a part of something.

The kid in him—the one that didn't want to risk his heart—said, *A few months isn't everything, but it's something.* Maybe it was the best life had for him, the best he could hope for.

The risk taker whispered, *But what if it's not?*

* * *

Jules sat in church next to Cam, acutely aware that his arm was touching hers from shoulder to elbow. Her hands were twisted in her lap and she hadn't heard a word the pastor said. She kept replaying last night's conversation in her mind.

She'd told him she loved him. But what was that ill-defined emotion that flitted across his face? Was it shock? Was it relief?

Who knew?

Certainly not her.

The sound of the organ jolted her from her thoughts. Was the sermon over? She jumped to her feet along-side the rest of the people in her pew and opened her hymnal, not even sure what page she was supposed to be on. She caught up to the page and stanza at right about the time everyone else closed their hymnals and Pastor Doug said the benediction. Finally. Sitting next to Cam and not knowing what he was thinking was torture.

She had to escape. "I'm gonna run to the nursery and get the girls."

"I've got to pick up Levi, anyway, so I'll get Elea-nor and Emma, too," Jordan said. She hurried down the aisle to the back door of the sanctuary before Jules could even get a word out.

"What in the world?" Jordan wasn't even going toward the nursery. Jules started that direction, but found herself flanked by Claire and Wynn, who locked arms with her. She glanced around for Cam and saw the back of his head, as he was being escorted out of the sanctuary by Latham.

It was starting to sink in that this was no ordinary

Sunday after church with them all heading out to the farm for family lunch. She pinned her sister with a look. "What's going on? And don't say nothing."

"My lips are sealed," Wynn laughed and continued to drag Jules toward the double doors that led to the fellowship hall. Once there, she and Claire each took a door handle and pulled the doors open.

Jules found herself staring at a wedding shower wonderland. There were streamers and flowers and gleaming silver trays, pretty party food and at least twenty beaming women.

Jules said, through teeth clenched into a smile, "I'm going to kill you."

"Not worried. Too many witnesses. And don't worry about the kids. We asked the nursery ladies to stay." Wynn led her to a table full of food and turned her loose, clearly of the opinion that a cucumber sandwich might help her mood.

Despite feeling like a huge fraud, Jules was so touched. The table was covered with plates and dishes holding cucumber finger sandwiches, lemon squares, tiny brownies with powdered sugar, chicken salad on shaped bread. She'd attended scores of luncheons just like this one. And as always, the offerings so lovingly prepared underscored Jules's certainty that food was comforting. It made people happy.

She turned to the small crowd of ladies standing by, who were watching her with love shining on their faces. These were the women who had watched her grow up, come to her high school graduation, held her hand when she was grieving her dad.

"Y'all. I can't even…" She reached for their hands.

"I don't know what to say. Thank you so much for doing this. What a sweet, sweet surprise."

"Fix a plate," Mrs. Matthews said. "We're starving."

The ladies standing around her laughed. Mrs. Norris nodded. "It's true. Pastor Doug can preach a long sermon."

Jules picked up one of the clear plastic plates. She loaded it with food and sat at one of the round tables, which the ladies had decorated with beautiful old lanterns adorned with roses and ivy from their own gardens.

Molly and Janice, a couple of her friends from high school, joined her. They talked about kids and preschool and which kid had which teacher at the moment. Her friend Molly asked whether she was going to sign Eleanor up for T-ball. *T-ball?*

Jules lifted her eyebrows. "Now I know you're teasing me. They don't really play sports at three, do they?"

"Oh, yeah, they do. And it's serious business."

Feeling like a dark cloud just parked itself over her head, Jules said, "Girl, I've barely got my head above water as it is."

Her friend Janice set her pink lemonade on the table. "That's the thing no one tells you about being a mom. Everyone feels that way. Like you're spinning plates and they're all about to fall, all the time."

Molly nodded. "At least we had time to get used to the chaos before we added number two. You got two at once. A baby *and* a toddler."

Janice widened her eyes, leaning forward conspiratorially. "How do you think Elaine Calvin is doing? Did you hear she had triplets?"

"No!" Jules put her fork down on the table. "I haven't heard any news since the bakery's been closed, too."

Janice's and Molly's eyes met across the table. Janice said, "We peeked in the window when we were out walking the other day. It looks so great in there. We totally can't wait for you to open back up."

"Oh, you guys. That makes me feel so good. I'm glad you're excited about it. I can't wait for you to see the new menu."

One of the older ladies who'd been friends with Jules's mom for years dinged her water glass to get everyone's attention. "Jules, we just wanted you to know how much we love you and how thrilled we are that you're happily married."

The uneasy sensation in Jules's tummy was back with a vengeance. She was married, at least. That much was true.

Mrs. Jackson continued, "We know you don't need all the usual shower items, so we pooled our resources and did something a little different for you and we hope you'll enjoy it. We wish you all the best, hon."

Claire set a small square basket filled with tissue and envelopes in front of Jules, who lifted one from the basket and opened it. Inside, she found four tickets to Bellingrath Gardens. *Oh.*

The next envelope held four tickets to the nearby zoo. The next, a family membership to the kids' science museum.

Each envelope held an experience, a way for their family to enjoy spending time together. Jules could never have imagined a more perfect gift. She had to wonder if they would be using them as a family of four, or if Cam would be off on his next adventure by the time they used the tickets.

She loved him. Now she had to trust that it was enough.

She sighed, but smiled and stood so she could address the small group of ladies. "You guys have no idea how much this means to me. Our family was formed, I guess you could say, a little unconventionally."

That comment got a chuckle from the ladies around the room.

"But your support and love and joy in celebrating with us means the world to me. Thank you." Jules made her way to the door, and as the ladies gathered their trays and started for home, she hugged each one and thanked her personally.

Later, as she went to the nursery to pick up the girls, she couldn't help wondering what had happened to Cam and if he'd had a similar ambush.

And if he had that same uneasy feeling in the pit of his stomach that she did.

While Jules was eating finger sandwiches with her friends from high school, Cam, Ash and Latham were eating barbecue with the husbands, some of whom Cam remembered vaguely from middle school. "It was nice of you guys to take me out to lunch."

"It was either this or go to the shower with the women. I'm not into food I have to eat twenty of to make an actual adult-size portion. Plus, sausage balls don't count as actual meat." Ash held up a rib. "This is meat."

Cam grinned as he bit into his own barbecued rib. He'd never had friends like Juliet's brothers before. He'd never had friends. Not really.

His smile faded. This life he'd walked into was even better than he'd imagined it. The girls had stolen his heart. The house he'd bought had become a home to him, maybe the first he'd ever really had. The woman he'd married…she wasn't perfect, even though she'd like to be.

She had a blind spot. She loved him.

He let a slow breath out. She'd shocked him last night and he hadn't slept much, with her declaration running through his mind. Running through his heart—like streams of water in the desert.

"I've been elected to say a few words. Or actually, I think as the most recent newlywed, I drew the short straw." Latham cleared his throat. "So, Cam, we're all very happy to have you in the family, especially because you are a beast on the soccer field. You lucked out when Jules decided to marry you. She's a keeper and you got me and Ash and Joe as brothers-in-law. Congratulations."

There were chuckles around the table as Latham pulled an envelope from his front jacket pocket and handed it across the table to Cam.

"What's this?" Cam wiped his hands on a napkin, took the envelope and slid his finger under the flap. He stared down at the card. It was a voucher for three days in Gatlinburg, in a penthouse suite. He looked up. "Guys, I don't know what to say."

Ash grinned. "We know you and Jules didn't get to have a honeymoon and this isn't much, but it will get you out of town for a few days. We've arranged for Mrs. Matthews to watch the girls for you. You'll just have to let her know the dates."

"We'd have liked to send you off to Europe or the Caribbean or something, but let's face it, we're too poor for that." Latham laughed. "Oh, and Joe pitched in, too."

"Joe pitched in for what?" Cam's other brother-in-law stood in the door, gold police chief badge clipped prominently to his waist. Cam couldn't see the service weapon, but he assumed it was under the jacket, too.

"The honeymoon," Cam said. "And thank you. All of you. It means a lot."

"Cam, can we have a minute in private?" Joe asked, his face set in serious, hard lines, his eyes sheltered by silver-lensed aviators.

Cam paused in the middle of sliding the gift into his jacket pocket. "Of course."

He followed Joe outside the small restaurant. There was a warm, soft breeze blowing, one of those early spring days in the South when it felt more like summer. Cam couldn't think of anything he'd done wrong, but still he felt uncomfortable, a brief irrational sense that he'd been "found out" in some way.

"Joe, is Jules okay? The girls?"

"Yes, they're fine. I'm sorry if I worried you."

Cam frowned. "What's this about, then?"

Joe slid his sunglasses off. "It's about your mother. There's been a development."

A development? Cam searched Joe's face and found no clue. He crossed his arms and waited, because he knew one thing: it couldn't be good news.

Chapter Sixteen

Unmoving, Cam stared at the badge on his brother-in-law's waist. "What about my mother?"

"She's been arrested by federal marshals for credit card fraud, among other things. She's being held at the county jail until her detainment hearing, which is probably on Monday. I thought you and Jules would want to know." Joe's words and face were expressionless. It obviously wasn't his first time dealing with the family of someone accused of a crime, and the chief of police in their little town was definitely aware of Cam's difficult history with Vicky.

"I appreciate you coming out here to let me know."

Joe hesitated. "I don't know if you have any experience with this kind of thing, but there's a good chance someone from the federal defender's office will call you to see if you will vouch for her in court. They might even ask if she can live in your home until trial."

The idea of it was a slap of reality. "I'm not putting the girls in jeopardy for her. Not when she was willing to use them for money."

"I understand. Family can be hard. I'm sorry you're having to deal with this."

Cam shook Joe's hand. "Thanks for bringing it to my attention."

He walked back inside the restaurant and stuck his head into the private room where they'd been eating. "Fellas, I'm gonna have to go, but it was fun. Great meal, great company. And thanks again for the card."

During the smattering of congratulations that followed, his phone buzzed in his pocket, but Cam didn't look at it, not until he walked to his car, got in and closed the door. Then he turned the phone in his hand so he could see the readout. It was a number he didn't recognize, but he assumed it was about his mother.

He couldn't ignore the call forever—there was no one else to be responsible for her—but he could wait.

Rolling down the window, letting the warm air buffet his face, he took a deep breath. There were so many ramifications from Vicky's arrest. The first and most important was that the girls would now be safe from the specter of being raised by their grandmother.

But the second… Juliet had married him to keep the girls safe. Now that the question of custody was resolved, Cam was left with an even bigger one. Would Jules realize she'd made a mistake? And would she want him, now that she didn't need him?

Jules had the mixer going and an array of spices open in front of her, trying to decide which ones she wanted to combine in these carrot cake muffins. They needed to look like muffins and taste like cake. Oh, maybe a cream cheese filling. She made a note on the recipe, her heart rate picking up speed when she heard the garage door open.

When Cam walked into the room, she was happy to see him, but she felt something else. Wariness. She'd bared her soul to him last night, and even though she'd told him she didn't want him to say anything, she desperately wanted him to say *something*.

Anything. Anything to stop the flood of random thoughts through her mind.

He leaned against the counter, looking weary. His collar was unbuttoned, his tie already loosened, but he pulled it the rest of the way off, looping it in his hand. "How was the ladies' party?"

She pointed to the basket of cards she'd left on the kitchen table with the girls' diaper bags and sippy cups. "They gave us gift certificates to stuff we can do as a family."

Cam let that process for a minute. He nodded. "Nice."

"How was the guys' party?"

He pulled an envelope out of his coat pocket and tapped it. "They gave us a honeymoon."

"A honeymoon?" The flush started on her chest, and she could feel it creeping up her cheeks. Spending a weekend alone with him, without the girls as a buffer, especially after what she'd said last night? How much humiliation could she take? Would he go that far to keep up appearances?

"In Gatlinburg, so we don't have to be gone from the girls too long. They even arranged for Mrs. Matthews to babysit," he laughed. "Or at least, their wives did. I can't imagine the guys coming up with this idea."

"That sounds fun. Listen, Cam, about our conversation last night—"

He stopped her with a hand on her arm. "Before we talk about that, I have news."

Jules could hear the seriousness in his voice. She turned the mixer off, knowing the batter was probably hopelessly overworked by now, anyway. "What's going on?"

"Joe came by the restaurant. He was working, but he wanted to tell me that my mother was arrested on Friday afternoon. Federal charges, so he didn't have to be the one to arrest her, thankfully."

Her hand crept up to cover her mouth, her eyes never leaving his.

"She's going to spend some time in prison. It's only a matter of time. There's a possibility she could get out at the detention hearing, but it's not likely unless I vouch for her and give her a place to live, and that isn't happening. Not as long as I'm responsible for Emma and Eleanor's safety."

Her heart was beating so fast and so hard Jules found it hard to breathe.

It was over.

The worry, the anguish. The late nights on her knees. The very real fear that she would be disappointing her best friend by not protecting her babies.

She threw herself into Cam's arms. "I can't believe it's over. I can't believe it." He looked down at her, his green eyes soft, and suddenly she remembered that it was over only because his mother was likely going to prison. "Cam, I'm sorry. I wasn't thinking."

He crushed his lips to hers and she felt every thought leave her head but one. Him.

His hand caressed her hair, teasing one lock loose from her hair band. "You're too good for me, Juliet."

She looked up into his eyes and shook her head. "No. Just good enough."

He still hadn't said the words she wanted to hear, and his eyes darkened, even though his arms were still wrapped around her. "Are you sure you want this in your life, Juliet? As long as she knows where I am, she will always want something."

"I want you in my life," she said simply.

And she hoped that it really was that simple.

Eleanor came to the door of the kitchen. Cam released Jules and lifted the sleep-heavy three-year-old into his arms, and she nestled her head on his shoulder.

He looked over at Jules, then out at the pond in the backyard. "Do you think we could go fishing after supper?"

With a shriek, Eleanor pulled in the first fish. She couldn't figure out the reeling, so she just turned and ran, Pippi running and barking beside her, until she dragged the flopping bass onto the bank. Then she promptly let go of the rod and the fish splashed back into the water.

Cam was laughing so hard he couldn't see, but he managed to pull in her fish. Gingerly, he wrapped his fingers around it and removed the hook. "Do you want to see it, Eleanor?"

Eleanor took two steps toward him, closed her eyes and held her finger out. He touched the fish to her outstretched finger. She squealed again and stomped her feet. "Ew, yucky!"

Jules laughed. "I guess she's not going to be our fisherman."

She'd spread a quilt on the grass, but she wasn't doing much sitting. Instead she was chasing their new walker. Emma thought it was hilarious to toddle as fast as she could toward the water, calling, "Mama, Mama," in her husky little voice.

"You come back here, Emma Louise," Jules said.

Emma stopped short and nearly toppled over into the pond, but she managed to maintain her balance. He laughed again. These girls were his heart.

The toddler looked up at Cam with a wicked gleam in her eye. "Dada."

Eleanor had been calling him Daddy off and on since the night of the preschool fund-raiser, but Cam figured that with her, it was more the fact that she saw him as the father figure in their little family.

Emma saw him as *Daddy* and that knocked him as off balance as he would've been if the ground beneath him had shifted.

She lifted one foot and scrunched up her tiny toes. He arranged his features into an I-mean-business face. She took a step, putting that foot down and picking up the other one, teasing him. He put the mock-warning tone in his voice. "Emma…"

She turned away from the water and ran from him, slaying him with her laughter. He chased her down and scooped her into his arms, then tossed her into the air and pretended to gobble her up as she laughed until she hiccuped.

He set her down on her feet and she promptly re-played the whole scenario.

Thirty minutes later, after another dozen fish and at least twice that of Emma being caught just before disaster, both girls had worn themselves out and the sun was sinking quickly in the sky, the temperature dropping with it. Emma was sound asleep on her back on the quilt, her bottle sliding out of her hand, the puppy curled up against her side. Eleanor was in Cam's lap, mumbling about fish, her eyes drooping.

He sighed, but not in disappointment. It was contentment he was feeling. Peace. He snuggled Eleanor closer, shifting her so she could lay her head on his chest. He said softly to Jules, "I used to think it was the big things that mattered most, but now I don't think that's true. I think a life—a real life, a happy life—is made from a collection of small moments that add up to something big."

He glanced at Juliet sitting beside him in the swing, her blond ponytail a long curl over her shoulder.

It wasn't the first time he'd felt peace. In his travels, he'd experienced it—looking out over a lush green valley from the peak of a mountain, or feeling the rush of wind and the vastness of the atmosphere when skydiving.

He'd scraped together a patchwork of peaceful memories that made up his life, much like that quilt Emma was sleeping on.

But this—this was something different. He put his arm around Juliet, dropping a kiss on her head. He opened his mouth to say *I love you*, but the words wouldn't form.

Instead he heard the words she'd spoken earlier. *Just good enough.*

Juliet Sheehan had never settled for just good enough in her entire life. She demanded perfection for herself and for everything she did. So why was she suddenly willing to settle?

A fresh wave of doubt crashed the pocket of peace he'd found this afternoon, shattering it. Maybe it had all been an illusion, like the illusion that they were happy. Like the illusion that they were a family.

He hugged Eleanor closer to his chest and stood. "I'm going to take her inside and tuck her in bed."

Jules smiled up at him. "Sweet girl. She's had a busy day. I'll be up with Emma in a few minutes. It's getting chilly out here and we have a big day tomorrow. I'll be leaving before dawn to get ready for the menu tasting tomorrow night."

"I'll manage the girls in the morning." A statement that would've been so foreign to him even a few months before, but now Cam was adept at bottles and diapers and three-year-old hair bows.

The sleepy puppy stood and yawned before following Cam across the yard and into the house. As Cam closed the door, he could see Juliet silhouetted in the swing, one foot tucked underneath her. He wondered what she was thinking, and if her thoughts followed his. Was she wishing things were different? Or wishing they could stay the same?

Cam had married her for the sake of the children. Maybe he should leave her for her own sake. He didn't doubt that Juliet believed she loved him, but would there come a day when settling for the life that had been chosen for her wouldn't be enough?

He knew he should lay it all on the table and give

her a choice, a real choice, like she'd given him when she'd asked him to marry her.

He just didn't know if he was strong enough to do it.

Chapter Seventeen

The next morning, Cam found himself with two little early risers. Early risers who'd been fed and dressed and were bored with their toys with an hour still to pass before preschool started.

Eleanor's tablet needed charging, a fact that had her searching for entertainment, which mostly consisted of annoying her sister and the dog. She tried to annoy Cam, but when he refused to be baited, she went for shock and awe, dumping her juice all over the brand-new carpet in the living room.

"Eleanor!"

She scowled at him and released the cup, sending it splashing into the pool of apple juice.

He picked the baby up from the floor, buckled her into her infant car seat and pointed at the garage door. "Let's go. Now, Eleanor."

"Where we going?" His niece frowned at him and crossed her arms. She stopped short of stomping her patent leather–clad foot in the puddle of juice, but just barely.

"To the park." Anything to save his sanity. Cam

grabbed their diaper bags from the hook and opened the door. He wasn't sure what had gotten into Eleanor, except for the fact that three-year-olds were apparently moody little creatures. He'd heard Claire refer to one of her toddlers as a three-nager but hadn't understood the reference. Until now.

He snapped Emma's seat into its base in the back seat of the van, then lifted Eleanor into her seat on the other side and buckled her in. He touched her nose. "All set."

The playground in Red Hill Springs was right behind the library, so Cam pulled into the parking lot there and unloaded the girls. A few minutes later, both of them were cheerfully swinging in the toddler swings. He wasn't sure how long it would last, but for the moment, at least, they were happy.

He was just down the street from the café, where Juliet would be preparing the staff and prepping for the night's menu tasting. She'd be making last-minute adjustments, and he imagined that, even though she was in her element, she'd be feeling nervous.

She didn't need to worry. He'd done a last walk-through on Friday. Her vision for the Hilltop had come to life and it was amazing. They would have their party tonight, with the tasting menu, and if all went according to plan, she'd be opening the café to the public a week from today.

"Higher!" Eleanor kicked her feet. He obliged, giving both her and Emma another push before going around in front of them to tickle their toes and make them squeal.

Cam laughed and replayed the scenario again. And again. It was such nice weather, he was glad he'd gotten the girls out of the house. People were walking on the track that circled the grassy area where he and the guys played soccer on Saturdays. In the field today, a mom was coaching her preschooler on how to hit a baseball off a tee.

It was the kind of scene that made a person who'd spent the majority of his adult life outside the country feel a little patriotic, a little apple pie and ice cream. He grinned at the thought. Small-town life was making him sentimental.

He glanced up and noticed a woman on the porch of the library staring at them. She was holding her cell phone up at an angle that almost looked like she was taking pictures of him with the girls. That was strange.

He was used to getting some curious looks—after all, he was a well-known author and people often recognized him, even if they didn't remember from where. But this was different. The skin prickled on the back of his neck.

"It's time to go, girls. Eleanor, time to go to school."

"No!" His niece screamed the word.

He picked Emma up from the swing and tried to figure out how he was going to get Eleanor out without her cooperation. He finally figured he couldn't, not while holding Emma. He placed the toddler on her feet, waiting for her to find her balance, then turned back to Eleanor.

"Come on, El. We've got to go."

She grabbed hold of the chains. "I don't wanna go!"

Well, so much for his hopes of not causing a scene. A couple moms with strollers had slowed their morning walks and were watching the action unfold as Eleanor screamed and Emma toddled off.

"Emma, come back, honey." He had to get out of here. Sweat beaded across his forehead. There was nothing to be done but to peel Eleanor's fingers from the chains one by one. He lifted her from the seat and she kicked him square in the solar plexus. His breath rushed out with an *oomph*.

And Emma was halfway to the slides.

With Eleanor still flailing in his grasp, he ran toward Emma, scooped her into his other arm and headed for Juliet's minivan in the parking lot.

Eleanor screamed, "Stop it! You're not my dad!"

He went hot. *Perfect.*

"You're not my dad!"

The moms were gawking and the woman on the library porch had her phone to her ear. He struggled toward the minivan, trying desperately not to drop one of the kids. It was only about fifty feet away, but it seemed like a mile, with Eleanor squirming in his arms.

He stepped off the grass and into the parking lot—almost there—just as two black-and-white patrol cars pulled up, blocking his path. One of the officers got out and walked toward him. The other stayed behind the open door to his patrol car, his hand on his unsnapped weapon.

Cam's skin went clammy. He knew he hadn't done anything wrong, but in his mind, he was catapulted back in time to the fifteen-year-old kid who lost his whole family over a handful of dollars and some change.

He tried to tell himself he was a professional now, respected in his field, but the cops didn't know that.

Cam pushed back against the overwhelming feeling of being "found out," even though no crime had been committed.

"Sir, keep your hands where we can see them."

Eleanor stopped struggling and stared at the cop, her little dark eyebrows folding into a scowl. He hitched her up into a more secure position on his hip. "Can I help you?"

"We got a call that there might be a kidnapping situation in the park. Are these your children?" The cop looked at Cam with suspicion, his weight shifting, body tense and ready to react.

Cam's heart thundered in his chest, adrenaline spiking, sending the message to his muscles: *Run. Get himself to safety—get the girls to safety.* He knew rationally that running was the absolute wrong thing to do, but his body was telling his mind something different.

He narrowed his focus. *Stay present. Here and now. Answer the question.* "The girls are my nieces."

Eleanor took the small lull in conversation as her cue to start screaming again. "Don't wanna go! Don't wanna go!"

The cop's right eyebrow shot up, his skeptical gaze traveling between Cam's brown skin and the girls' peaches-and-cream complexions. Cam sighed. "Their mother was my half sister. Different fathers."

He could barely keep his grip on the children as Eleanor kicked and Emma squirmed to get down. "Look, this is not a great time to have a discussion about my parentage. I appreciate your concern for the girls' safety, but I need to get them to preschool. Sir."

He took a step toward his car and the officer

jumped forward, one hand out, the other hovering over his weapon. "Stop right there. We're not done yet."

At the harsh tone, Emma started to cry. Eleanor, for all her screaming to get down, couldn't scramble back into his embrace fast enough. She huddled against him, her wet face pressing into his shirt. A slow anger started to burn in Cam's gut and he tamped it down. He could not let anger show on his face or in his own body language.

The girls' safety was at stake.

He lifted his hands the best he could with Emma and Eleanor in his arms. "Okay, okay...*okay.* I'm not going anywhere."

Cam realized a small crowd had gathered to watch the commotion, adding to the danger and humiliation. At least one of them was filming with her phone, which escalated everything and put the girls at further risk.

He took a deep breath and willed his shoulders to relax. "We can settle this with one phone call. Just call your boss. Chief Sheehan is my brother-in-law. I'm married to his sister Juliet, and these are her kids. *Our* kids."

The two cops exchanged a look and the one closest to him nodded for the other one to make the call. Cam couldn't hear much except for a lot of "Yes, sirs" and a final "Copy that." The officer ended the call, put his phone in his pocket and walked over to Cam, a jerk of his head sending the other police officer back to his car.

"I'm very sorry to inconvenience you, Mr. Quinn. You have my apologies, the apologies of the Red Hill Springs Police Department and the personal apology of Chief Sheehan." The young cop's face was ruddy, sweat breaking out across his forehead. "It was our mistake."

"I'd just like to go now."

When the officer stepped aside, Cam opened the door to the van with his key fob and buckled the girls into their car seats as fast as humanly possible. Emma was still crying, a pitiful soft keening. He tucked a pacifier in her mouth and her wails turned to sniffles. He rubbed sweaty curls away from her forehead. "It's okay. You're okay, baby."

Inside he was seething. Those people had put him and the girls in a humiliating, if not dangerous, situation. What if he hadn't had the chief of police as his brother-in-law? What then?

He sat in the driver's seat and tried to start the car, but his hands were shaking too badly. *Sorry to* inconvenience *you?* While one officer had stood there with his hand on his gun? He'd been scared out of his mind that something would happen and he wouldn't be able to protect the girls.

Unfortunately, this kind of thing was all too common. He thought about the woman on the porch of the library, ready and waiting with her phone before Eleanor even kicked up a fuss. He was lucky it had ended the way it did.

Eleanor was silent in the back, staring blankly at the seat in front of her. He'd give anything to turn back time and stay at home, where her biggest problem was that her tablet wasn't charged.

His heart ached.

And that wave of doubt he'd felt the night before was now more like a tsunami. Those police officers hadn't seen a professional author. They hadn't seen *him.* He may as well have been the fifteen-year-old kid with a mayonnaise jar full of one-dollar bills.

He lowered his head to the steering wheel. How could he ever hope to be enough for them if a simple trip to the park was impossible?

How could he ever hope to be enough?

The café was sparkling tonight. Their guests were oohing and aahing over the newly remodeled space and the deck beyond, where a cozy fire burned in the outdoor fireplace.

Jules slid through the crowd, accepting compliments and congratulations. She'd prepared the workers in the kitchen well and they were replenishing the trays on the long counter, which held bite-size pieces of the food that would be on the regular menu at the Hilltop when they opened next week. She wanted the people in attendance to leave craving more, so that they would come back.

"Jules." Jordan, wearing a hot-pink maternity shirt, jeans and cowboy boots, grabbed her by the elbow. "I need this chicken salad in my life."

Jules laughed. "I'm glad you like it. I'll bring you the leftovers tomorrow. Hey, Jordan, have you seen Cam?"

Jordan looked up from her plate in surprise. "He's not here yet? He was dropping the girls off at the farm to spend the night with Amelia when I left there an hour ago."

"Thanks." Jules paused. "How's Maisey?"

"Due to foal any day now, which is why I went out to check on her. And no, the irony's not lost on me that my horse and I are both as big as the side of a house at the moment."

Jules laughed again. "This, too, shall pass. I'll see you later. Try the mini cupcakes. The pecan pie flavor is the best one."

Her sister-in-law flashed her a wide smile. "Thanks for the tip."

Where was Cam? There was no way he would miss this if something hadn't happened. It was every bit as much his night as hers.

She stepped out onto the deck. Under the warm glow of the string lights, a group of people stood gathered around the fire. None of them was Cam.

She turned around, straining to identify each face in her restaurant, a shiver of worry forming in her stomach.

"You're a huge success, sis." Joe stepped up beside her as he popped a mini red velvet cupcake into his mouth.

"Thank you. It's surprising, actually, how right it feels. I wish Mom was here. Two months feels like forever." Her eyes still searched for a glimpse of Cam.

"She'll be home soon enough and giving you advice you don't need."

"That's so true. I'll be wishing she'd go back to Hawaii after a couple of weeks."

Joe put his hand on her arm. "Listen, I just wanted to apologize personally for what happened today. Are the girls okay?"

She slowly raised her eyes to meet her brother's, her body going cold. "What happened today?"

"Oh, man, I figured you already knew. Cam was at the park with the girls this morning before school.

The librarian got it in her head that he'd kidnapped them and called 911."

Jules took a deep breath before she said slowly, "But he's their dad, so when he told them who he was, they left, right?"

Joe's gaze flicked away and back. "Not exactly. Eleanor was apparently having a bad morning. She was kicking and screaming as Cam was carrying her out of the park."

"Like any toddler does when they don't want to leave the park. What *happened*, Joe?"

"Cam tried to get in the van and two of my officers stopped him. He had to get them to call me before they'd let him take the girls to school."

"I have to go." She couldn't breathe. She had to get out of here and get to Cam, because she had a bad feeling she knew why he wasn't here. And what he was going to do.

"Jules, wait," her brother called after her. *"Jules."*

Cam was going to leave. She knew in her gut that, after what happened this morning, he'd let that crazy idea take root in his head. He'd tell himself that they were better off without him. And he would leave.

She ran through her beautiful, pristine kitchen— the kitchen that Cam had helped her design—and grabbed her purse off her desk in the office.

Lanna appeared in the doorway. "What's going on?"

"Something's happened and I have to go. I'll be back as soon as I can. I'm so sorry, Lanna."

Her friend and acting manager of the Hilltop opened the back door for her. "Go. I'll cover for you."

Jules flew down the street to where her car was

parked, praying she would get there before he left, praying she could say the right words to convince him to stay. But for that to happen, he had to believe that love was enough to conquer fear and shame and prejudice.

He had believe that love was *enough*.

Chapter Eighteen

Cam shoved a few shirts and a pair of jeans into his bag, although he didn't know why he was bothering. He had his wallet and his passport and that was really all he needed. He'd spent years going from place to place with a bag and a camera. He could do it again.

He glanced at his watch. He had at least another hour before Jules got home with the girls, but he wanted to be gone before she got home. Before she had the chance to try to spin what happened today into something that didn't change things for all of them. Maybe it was a cowardly thing to do, but he knew if he looked in her eyes, he might never have the strength to leave.

He'd written them a letter. For a person who'd made a career out of using words, he'd failed miserably at putting his feelings on paper. He'd wished for a home, a family. He'd seen it in his mind the first time he'd set foot in this house. And for a moment he'd had it, all that he'd dreamed of, all that he'd never known he needed.

A picture Eleanor had drawn of their family lay

on the bed. Here was proof that they had existed—a mama with long blond hair, two little girls with dark curls, even a fat black puppy. But it was the daddy that drew his attention now—a tall daddy with brown skin and a big happy smile.

He wasn't smiling now. He carefully folded the picture and put it in his wallet.

From the door came a voice. "I heard what happened today."

He spun around, his heart constricting as he caught sight of Jules. "You haven't heard it from my perspective."

She stepped into the room, her long legs set off by slim black pants. "Then why don't you tell me about it?"

"No." He was frozen in place, his hand hovering over the handles of his bag. "It doesn't matter."

Her gaze snapped to his. "It matters to me."

She was still the most beautiful woman he'd ever seen. She walked—sauntered, really—to the desk under the window in his room. With one long finger, she slid the single piece of paper closer to her.

"Jules, please don't."

She raised one blond eyebrow. "Why not? This letter is to me, isn't it?"

"Yes, but—"

"But it wasn't meant to be read?"

He closed his eyes, took a deep breath and opened them again, giving her the truth. "It wasn't meant to be read in front of me."

"I see." She picked the letter up from the table and slowly walked back across the room, mile-high heels clicking on the hardwood floor. "It was meant to be read by me and the girls as we congratulated ourselves on our narrow escape from life with you."

It was then that he realized she wasn't worried or sad, she was coldly furious. "Jules—"

"Quiet, please, I'm reading. 'Dear Juliet, I'm sorry. We always knew it was only a matter of time.'" She looked up, caught his gaze with her own. "Is that what you were thinking all this time we've been married? Every time we had a conversation, every time we kissed? That it was only a matter of time? Because that's not what I was thinking."

"No, Jules. I wasn't. I was thinking I was the luck-iest man on the planet to get to be with the three of you every day." He moved then, closer to her, but not touching her. He didn't think she'd want him to. "I was thinking maybe if I just wanted it badly enough, I could make it last forever."

Her blue eyes filled with tears and, as she looked down at the letter again, one splashed onto the creamy-white paper. He was causing her pain and he couldn't bear it. He reached out for her, but once again pulled his hand back.

She straightened her shoulders and continued read-ing. "'I will think of you every minute of every day and if you ever need anything, you only need to ask.' This isn't worth the paper it's written on. You're such a liar."

He took a step back. "What?"

"Let me find it again and make sure I have the wording right. Yep, yep. Here it is." She ran her fin-gers over the words. "'If you ever need anything, you only need to ask.' Well, we do need something, Cam.

You're taking away the thing we need most. We need you."

His heart cracked, his chest burning with the need to pull her into his arms. He loved her. He'd been a fool to think not saying the words would somehow keep him from feeling it.

He loved her. And he was terrified he would never get over the loss of her.

He whispered, "You didn't see their faces."

She scoffed. "The cops? Who cares what they think?"

"Not the cops. The *girls*. They were traumatized, Jules. Emma was sobbing and Eleanor went from being the most irritating three-year-old in history to silently staring straight ahead with these gigantic tears rolling down her cheeks. I did that to them."

"That's not true."

"I may as well have. There's no getting around the fact that if I looked like you, no one would've called the cops. No one would've thought twice about it. They would have looked at Eleanor screaming and thought, 'We've all had those days.' Except that's not what happened. They looked at me and they saw a threat. And Emma and Eleanor were the ones who suffered because of it."

A tear spilled down her cheek. He wanted to grab her and hold her and tell her not to be sad, that he would fix everything. But he couldn't fix this.

And that was the whole point.

He needed to go. To pick up his bag and leave. But instead, he slid his hand into her hair. With one gentle tug, she was fitted against him, her eyes wide and dark and full of hurt. He leaned down and brushed his lips across hers. A salty, tear-streaked kiss full of regret and broken promises. He leaned his forehead against hers and whispered, "I'm sorry."

In the kitchen, Jules heard the garage door open and waited long seconds for the engine to start up. She imagined that Cam was sitting in his brand-new truck, at war with himself, wanting to stay but believing he needed to go.

She was so incredibly angry at him. She didn't agree with him. But that didn't mean she didn't understand his choice. *Dear God, please let him stay.*

But then she heard it. The roar of the V-8 engine in his truck pulling out and fading into the distance. He really was leaving.

Her phone buzzed on the counter and she picked it up. A text from Lanna. I've got the cleanup covered. It was a great night. I'm so proud of you, kiddo.

From the counter, she picked up the flyer they'd posted around town advertising the sneak peek at the new and improved Hilltop Café. This was supposed to be their big night together. They'd planned and prepared and planned some more.

And finally, tonight had been the payoff for all that hard work. She'd looked forward to coming home after the party and chatting about everyone's reaction to the remodel and the new menu. Because despite everything, she and Cam were friends.

She'd grown to depend on his ability to reason his way through a problem, and his easy camaraderie as they parented the girls. She closed her eyes. She couldn't even think about what it would mean for Emma and Eleanor that he was gone.

The phone buzzed in her hand again. She moved to silence it, but it was Claire, and the girls were with her at Red Hill Farm. "Claire?"

"Everyone's fine here," her sister-in-law said quickly. "I'm just calling to check on you. You'd left by the time I got to the menu tasting. And oh, Jules. Joe told me what happened today. I can't even imagine what the two of you must be going through."

Juliet took a deep breath and said it for the first time of what she imagined would be many times. "There's not going to be any 'two of us,' I'm afraid. Cam left."

There was silence on the other end of the call. Then, "Maybe all is not lost, Jules. I thought Joe and I were through, but we got a second chance. We gave each other a second chance."

"Maybe." It was nice of Claire to try to cheer her up, but Jules had laid her heart on the line and Cam had pretty much just stepped over it on the way out the door.

She crushed the flyer in her hand and threw it in the trash can.

Claire sighed. "I'm sorry. Listen, don't worry about the girls. They're sleeping and they're fine. Eleanor thought it was a grand adventure to have so many playmates around and Emma adores Amelia."

"Thanks, Claire. I'll pick them up in the morning."

As she hung up the phone, she heard a whimper. She'd been so distracted, she'd forgotten all about Pippi. When she opened the kennel door, the puppy shot out of it like she'd been fired by a cannon, all boneless wiggles and kisses. Opening the door, Jules followed the dog outside, sitting down on the steps to the yard while Pippi sniffed around.

She flipped through the pictures on her phone, pausing at the one from last night: a selfie of the four of them with Eleanor's fish. It was a tiny little thing, but El was so proud.

Cam was beaming. Even Emma was looking at the camera. It was a snapshot in time. A moment of happiness. She hadn't had any idea how fleeting it would be.

Pippi careened up the steps and pawed her way into Jules's lap. Jules rubbed the Lab puppy's ears and let her face drop into the soft black fur.

The phone buzzed again. She sighed but glanced at the readout, anyway. Nerves bloomed in her stomach. It was Patience Carter, the guardian ad litem for the girls. Juliet hesitated, not sure this was a call she wanted to answer, especially not tonight. But she slid her finger across the screen. "Hello?"

"Mrs. Quinn, it's Patience Carter. I'm calling because I've received some new information that we need to discuss. There was an accusation made against you and Mr. Quinn."

She put the dog down and stood. "Accusing us of what, exactly?"

"That your marriage was purely an attempt to maintain custody of the girls so you would have control over a life insurance policy they inherited from their parents."

Well, Jules didn't have to speculate who'd called in that anonymous tip. "Mrs. Carter, I assure you that's not the case."

"I'm glad to hear that. I do consider the source, but since I'll be the one signing the recommendation for custody, I want to make sure I have all the information I need before I make my report to the judge."

The law guardian's voice was crisp and efficient, even at nine o'clock at night. "Does tomorrow morning at eight work for you?"

"Of course, but the girls are spending the night with their cousins and Cam...is out of town."

"No problem. I'll see you then." The line went dead.

Jules stared at the phone, heart beating an anxious tattoo in her chest. She didn't need to worry. The GAL was being thorough, that was all.

She wondered for a minute if she should text Cam, but no. He'd made it clear that he was saying goodbye. He was afraid that his life would make theirs harder.

She just wished he knew that without him the sunshine would be a little bit dimmer. Their home emptier.

Their hearts broken.

Cam sped down the highway. His goal was to get to Atlanta tonight and to take the first plane in the morning out of there. He didn't care where. He just needed distance between himself and Red Hill Springs, Alabama.

From Juliet.

It wasn't real. None of it was real. He was a husband, a father, in name only. They'd gotten married for appearances. For the girls. For the judge. And he could tell himself that all day long.

He knew it wasn't true.

He loved her.

The man who didn't get involved, who bounced from adventure to adventure, never lingering long enough for complications, had stayed just a little too long.

And he'd left his heart behind.

He glanced in the mirror just in time to see red and blue lights flash on behind him. *Really, God?* Had he not had enough of dealing with the police today?

Cam slowly braked and waited until he found a place where he could safely pull over. His wallet was beside him, but he didn't dare reach for it in case an over-eager officer decided he was reaching for a weapon. He rolled the window down and put his hands—both hands—where they could be seen at the top of the steering wheel.

The huge cop walked toward Cam, silhouetted in the headlights of his patrol car, but then detoured around the truck. Maybe he wanted to be away from the street side?

The door opposite Cam opened and Joe slid into the passenger seat. "Hey."

Cam reared back against the driver's-side door. He took a deep breath and willed his heart rate to slow back to something closer to normal. He dropped his hands to his lap. At least he didn't have to be worried about being shot…he didn't think. "Aren't there rules about using your credentials for personal reasons?"

Joe shrugged. "Probably. But I wanted to talk to you in person."

"How'd you know where I'd be?"

"I didn't. I just took the fastest route to the largest airport within driving distance."

Cam frowned. "I knew I should've gone to New Orleans."

The lights from Joe's patrol car flashed, painting everything in sight red and blue. Fitting, actually, now that Cam thought about it. His whole day—his whole life—had been upended by the specter of those flashing lights.

Joe put his elbow on the ledge of the window. "I'm sorry about what happened today, Cam. If that's why you're leaving, I want you to know that I can personally guarantee that kind of thing will never happen again in my town."

"You can't protect them everywhere. I can't protect them at all, apparently."

"Ah." The single syllable seemed to imply understanding that Cam wasn't sure Joe had.

"You don't understand. You don't know who I am. I've done things, a lot of things, I'm not proud of. I wanted to leave that behind, remake the past with a future I'd dreamed of. I wanted the house and the family. And I thought I could make it fit with Jules and the girls. But she deserves so much better than me."

Joe frowned. "Maybe you're not giving Jules enough of a chance. Does she know all this stuff?"

Cam shifted in his seat. "She knows."

The big cop pinned Cam with an ice-blue stare. "And?"

"And I'm starting to see why you're good at interrogations."

Joe waited.

Cam lifted his hands and let them drop back to his lap. "And she says she doesn't care. But I don't think—"

"Do you love her?" His brother-in-law interrupted him.

"It doesn't matter."

"Do you *love* her? It's a simple question."

Cam sighed and ground his teeth. "Yes. I love her, but sometimes love isn't enough."

That elicited a low chuckle from his brother-in-law. "My friend, I've been down this road that you're traveling. It doesn't lead anywhere good."

Cam raised an eyebrow. "Well, the road you were on must've led you in a big loop because you ended up back with Claire."

Joe let out a bark of laughter before he sat back and looked at Cam thoughtfully. "When I told Jules what happened in the park today, she went flying out of the restaurant like her hair was on fire. Out of her own party, at the restaurant she brought to life. She doesn't care if you're perfect. She loves you."

He'd tried so hard to be the person he thought Jules would want him to be that he'd lost who *he* wanted to be. The words he'd said to Jules, the words that had haunted him for so many years, came back to him. *I'm the kid even a mother couldn't love.*

Cam had turned his back on Jules as surely as his mother had done to him so many years ago. He'd longed for her to stand up for him and she'd refused. And maybe his motives were better, but he'd turned his back just the same.

He'd spent his whole life running from the feeling that he wasn't worth fighting for. He wasn't going to do that to Jules and Emma and Eleanor. The love they shared—all of them shared—was worth going to the wall for. Maybe it wouldn't be easy and maybe he couldn't protect them from pain, but he could protect them from *this* pain.

Because he loved them and they were worth the fight.

He turned back to Joe. "I think maybe I'll be making a loop."

Joe looked up from his phone and smiled. "Glad to hear it. Why don't you follow me back to the farmhouse for the night? The girls are there. Jules will need you in the morning. Apparently someone told the guardian ad litem that you two got married only for the girls' money, and she wants some answers."

Jules was really angry at him. Angry enough that she hadn't messaged him about the meeting with the GAL in the morning. "That sounds like a meeting I should attend."

Cam wasn't going to let her down. She'd laid her heart out for him, risking everything, and he'd turned away. He wasn't going to do that again.

They needed him. And he needed them.

He just hoped he wasn't too late.

Chapter Nineteen

Jules threw the ball for Pippi, laughing as the puppy galloped across the lawn, slipping in the dew-covered grass. Fog rose in wispy curls over the surface of the pond. The sun was in a half state of wakefulness, just below the trees, sending its pink-and-gold light above the horizon. It was a baker's favorite hour, before the rest of the world was awake.

She wasn't worried about the guardian ad litem. She'd had a long talk with God and had been reminded that she'd prepared for this in every way she could. He would have the rest.

Claire had the girls for another few hours. The paperwork that proved Jules had put the life insurance money in a trust for the girls the very day it arrived was printed and in a neat file on the kitchen table. She had the copy of Glory and Sam's will, naming her as Emma and Eleanor's guardian. And she had the broken heart to prove that she'd actually fallen in love with Cam. Maybe it started out as an arrangement, but it hadn't ended that way.

Last night, she hadn't slept. Instead, she'd lain in

bed in the house she'd shared with Cam, replaying every minute of their conversation, as if she could somehow make the outcome different if she thought about it long enough and hard enough.

Pippi tilted her head, listening, then tore out of the yard toward the front of the house. Jules whistled and called her back, but the puppy had disappeared. She picked up her coffee mug and started after the dog, just in time to see Cam walk around the corner of the house, the pup dancing at his feet.

She caught her breath.

He looked so good—a little tired, but so handsome in his jeans and a lightweight sweater. His green eyes were brilliant in the soft light. He sent her a hesitant smile and she took a step forward.

But then she stopped. His leaving had left her raw and wary, and she wasn't ready to pretend nothing had happened. "Did the guardian ad litem call you?"

"Joe."

Her brother was meddling. "So you came back to meet with the GAL?"

"That, too. But I'm not here for the law guardian. I'm here for you."

Hope flared, a small flame, struggling to survive in the dark grief she'd felt when he left. She was trembling so hard she could barely get the words out. "You said goodbye."

"I did. I didn't get very far before I realized I was making a terrible mistake. I should never have left you, Jules. But I was so scared."

She looked up then, her eyes narrowing on his, searching them to find the truth. He *was* scared? Past tense?

"For most of my life, I've thought of myself as damaged—the kid even a mother couldn't love. I'd gotten good at hiding it, but I felt like the longer I was around people, the more likely they'd be to see the real me."

She'd suspected it, but hadn't known he realized it until now. Her heart broke a little more at the thought of what a lonely life that must've been. "That's why you only stay a few months in a place before you move on?"

He nodded. "I never thought I'd have someone who loved me unconditionally, a family, friends like your brothers."

"So we made a deal." Her words were an echo of the ones they'd spoken that night in the barn, but that night, the conversation had ended there.

"At first it was enough—it did seem like a dream, but the longer we were together, the more I knew it wasn't. It was real and it was *so* much better than I ever imagined it could be. And the better it got, the more scared I got. I was sure that it was all going to crumble around me."

She couldn't breathe. She wanted to reach out to him and tell him she'd never leave him, but she couldn't. Not yet.

Pippi flushed a bird from its roost in the bushes beside them. It took flight with a squawk and a rush of wings. Jules laughed, too loud, as she jumped.

Cam brushed her cheek with the backs of his fingers, an achingly tender touch, and she turned her face into the caress. She wanted to believe that he was home, that he'd come back to her. He wasn't the only one who was afraid of being hurt.

"I'm so sorry for last night. So sorry I left you." His words were soft, sincere.

"It was the incident in the park?" She reached up, tentatively, and touched his hand on her face with just her fingertips.

He nodded again and looked away, dropping his hand. "For months now, I've been living in fear that somehow I'd be found out, exposed for a fake. And yesterday, in the park, I knew I hadn't done anything wrong, but...there was a woman watching me the whole time we were at the playground. And when the cops came, there was a crowd of people around, filming and gawking."

"And it felt like they were all seeing you and all that you'd been trying to hide. And the girls were there, too, so that made it worse."

"How do you..." He pressed his fingertips to his forehead, the emotion he'd felt yesterday still there in the flutter of a blink, the tightness of his shoulders. "I should stop being surprised that you know me. I love you, Jules. I don't know how, but I think my heart recognized you the first time I saw you."

He stopped, laughed in surprise, and said it again. "I love you."

"I love you, too." A tear slid down her face and she impatiently swiped it away. "I don't need you to be anyone but who you are. You gave me the courage to go after my dream, too, but it's not a dream for me, unless you're here."

"You're not settling." It wasn't a question.

Her eyes were steady on his. "Juliet Sheehan Quinn does not settle."

A smile tugged at the corner of his mouth and she

leaned forward, kissing him just there. "I love you, Cam. I love every part of you—the author, the adventurer, the husband, the friend. We make each other's dreams come true."

She narrowed her eyes. "But if you ever decide to leave me again, you better pack four bags, because the girls and I are going with you."

He pulled her into his arms as the sun broke over the trees. Cupping her face with gentle, reverent hands, he kissed her—forehead, nose, eyelids, lips—whispering "I love you" with every touch.

And he was perfect. For her.

Epilogue

❧

Two years later

Cam guided Jules through the kitchen with his hands over her eyes. "Uh, you probably want to wait until after your surprise to look at the kitchen."

Of course she took that as a challenge and immediately tried to remove his hands.

"Seriously, Jules. It's not pretty."

"As long as something pretty came out of the oven when you all were through."

He thought about that for a minute. Kids, flour, cocoa, frosting. The whole thing was kind of a blur. "Yeah, no. Can't guarantee that, either."

She tripped over a dog bone and he steadied her on her feet. "Careful, now. We'll be in the hospital soon enough. No rushing the timetable."

"Hey, you're the one driving this—ahem—bus. Besides, you try being forty million years pregnant and then we'll talk." Jules laughed, and he loved the sound of it. He never took for granted that she was his. That this wonderful, awful, messy, beautiful life was his.

These days, he wasn't doing much adventure traveling. His travel books had shifted their focus and now he wrote about kid-friendly family destinations, and his adventure stories were for middle-grade readers.

From time to time, he still had the sense that he was living someone else's life, but he had an easy solution for that problem. All he had to do was try to take a nap and watch a little football. Before he knew it, there'd be a little boy using him as a trampoline or a little girl wanting him to check out her new princess shoes.

It *was* his life, and he loved it. "Now, big step over the threshold onto the deck."

The fancy deck furniture that came with the house had long since been replaced—with a picnic table that fit their ever-growing family.

Five-year-old Eleanor ran toward them, still wearing her soccer uniform from the morning's games. "Mama! We made you a cake!"

"Mama! Bir'day!" Emma was in her high chair at one end of the table.

"You made a cake? Oh, my goodness, what a surprise!"

Cam removed his hands from her eyes and she took in the whole tableau. The chocolate sheet cake with at least two boxes of candles on it, the frosting that had been tasted by many, many little fingers. He couldn't think about that too much.

But he knew Jules wouldn't have to think about it at all. It would be perfect.

* * *

The sound of sweet voices rose around Jules.
"Surprise!"
"Happy birthday!"

Despite herself, her eyes filled with tears. She and Cam were slowly but surely filling up all the rooms in their big house with kids. Kids who, like Cam, needed people who wouldn't turn their backs on them. She hadn't birthed any of their kids. Yet. But they were hers, just the same. And she loved them all so much.

"Happy birthday, Mom. Love you." Devon was their oldest—the shyest and quietest of the whole bunch. He and his four-year-old brother, Derek, had moved in with them a month before Devon turned eighteen, just before he aged out of foster care. He was theirs now, a permanent part of their family.

Maybe it seemed weird to some, to adopt a technical adult, but they didn't think so. Devon was one less orphan going through life believing he was unloved and unwanted.

And that had become Cam's mission, a mission Jules fully embraced.

Eleanor and Derek were now five, precocious and smart as little whips. Emma was three and so full of sass.

Their family drew stares wherever they went, their skin in shades of black, white and brown. But funny enough, when they'd stopped looking for the approval of everyone else, they'd stopped caring what anyone else thought. They found their worth somewhere else, in Someone else.

She sucked in a sharp breath as her belly tightened in a band of pain. "Hey, Cam."

Cam looked up. He must've seen something on her face because he was on his feet immediately. "Devon, buddy, I think you're gonna have to be in charge until Grandma Bertie gets here."

His eyes widened. "No problem. Don't worry, I got this."

Cam's strong hand was under Jules's elbow, helping her to rise. "I can bring my truck around for you."

Her laughed ended in a hiss. "As if I could get up into that thing."

Cam didn't laugh. And as she leaned into him, she could feel the tension lacing him. She looked up. "We're gonna be okay, babe," he whispered, his arms strong and firm around her.

The police lights flashed on as they turned from the driveway onto the highway. Cam squeezed her hand, but she knew he wasn't worried. This time, the two patrol cars weren't there for him, but for her. One cruiser sped around them, leading the way, and her brother Joe lifted a hand in silent salute.

Six hours later, a baby girl entered the world, all six pounds of her. The doctor gave her to Jules and she wrapped her arms around her brand-new baby girl, kissing her head.

She looked up at Cam, her eyes full of tears, but she didn't care. "I love you. We did this."

He shook his head, the awe on his face humbling her. "She's so beautiful. Do you think we should introduce her to the kids?"

Jules nodded and the nurse opened the door. Eleanor was the first one in, followed by Derek, then Devon, who was holding Emma.

Devon peered into the pile of blankets. "It's…cute."

Cam threw his head back and laughed. "It's a baby sister." He paused and said, "And her name is Gloriana."

They'd picked it as soon as they'd known Jules was having a girl. The name meant "glorious grace" and Jules thought it was perfectly fitting. It was God's grace that had brought Cam and Jules to love and God's grace that had brought their family together.

Jules looked up into Cam's beautiful ocean-green eyes. She whispered, "I love you."

He kissed her gently, with so much tenderness it almost broke her heart. "I know."

* * * * *

If you loved this story,
pick up the other books
in the Family Blessings series
from author Stephanie Dees:

The Dad Next Door
A Baby for the Doctor
Their Secret Baby Bond

Available now from Love Inspired!

Find more great reads at
www.LoveInspired.com.

Dear Reader,

Thanks so much for joining me in Red Hill Springs in *The Marriage Bargain*! When Jules appeared in her siblings' stories, I noticed that she always appeared to be perfect and calm, never a hair out of place. She just seemed to know where she was going and how to get there. In order for Jules to grow, I knew she was going to have to learn to deal with chaos, which came by way of two precious baby girls and their handsome uncle (who brought his own version of chaos to the party).

Over the course of the story, though Jules and Cameron struggle with different things, they both learn that their identities don't come from perfection or family or success or any of the other things we try to replace God with in our empty hearts.

Just like Cam and Jules, you have a Father who says that you were wonderfully made, who knew you before you were even born. I pray that you can rest in the knowledge that His opinion is the only one that matters and He loves you far beyond anything you can imagine.

I hope you've enjoyed your time with the Sheehan siblings in the Family Blessings series. For more information about upcoming books, please visit www.stephaniedees.com, or find me on Facebook at www.Facebook.com/authorstephaniedees.

Warmly,
Stephanie

Get 4 FREE REWARDS!

We'll send you 2 FREE Books plus 2 FREE Mystery Gifts.

Love Inspired® books feature contemporary inspirational romances with Christian characters facing the challenges of life and love.

FREE
Value Over
$20

YES! Please send me 2 FREE Love Inspired® Romance novels and my 2 FREE mystery gifts (gifts are worth about $10 retail). After receiving them, if I don't wish to receive any more books, I can return the shipping statement marked "cancel." If I don't cancel, I will receive 6 brand-new novels every month and be billed just $5.24 for the regular-print edition or $5.74 each for the larger-print edition in the U.S., or $5.74 each for the regular-print edition or $6.24 for the larger-print edition in Canada. That's a savings of at least 13% off the cover price. It's quite a bargain! Shipping and handling is just 50¢ per book in the U.S. and 75¢ per book in Canada.* I understand that accepting the 2 free books and gifts places me under no obligation to buy anything. I can always return a shipment and cancel at any time. The free books and gifts are mine to keep no matter what I decide.

Choose one: ☐ **Love Inspired® Romance Regular-Print** (105/305 IDN GMY4) ☐ **Love Inspired® Romance Larger-Print** (122/322 IDN GMY4)

Name (please print)

Address   Apt. #

City   State/Province   Zip/Postal Code

Mail to the **Reader Service:**
IN U.S.A.: P.O. Box 1341, Buffalo, NY 14240-8531
IN CANADA: P.O. Box 603, Fort Erie, Ontario L2A 5X3

Want to try 2 free books from another series? Call 1-800-873-8635 or visit www.ReaderService.com.

LI19R

"I wanted to talk to you about a project I'm getting started on. I'm opening a bakery."

"You are?" Annie couldn't keep the surprise out of her voice.

"Ja," Caleb said. "I stopped by to see if you'd be interested in working for me."

"You want to hire me? To work in your bakery?"

"I've had some success selling bread and baked goods at the farmers' market in Salem. Having a shop will allow me to sell year-round, but I can't be there every day and do my work at the farm. My sister Miriam told me you'd do a *gut* job for me."

"It sounds intriguing," Annie said. "What would you expect me to do?"

"Tend the shop and handle customers. There would be some light cleaning. I may need you to help with baking sometimes."

"Ja, I'd be interested in the job."

"Then it's yours. If you've got time now, I'll give you a tour of the bakery, and we can talk more about what I'd need you to do."

"Gut." The wind buffeted her, almost knocking her from her feet.

She mumbled that she needed to let her twin, Leanna, know where she was going. He wrapped his arms around himself as another blast of wind struck them.

"Hurry…anna…" The wind swallowed the rest of his words as she rushed toward the house.

She halted midstep.

Anna?

Had Caleb thought he was talking to her twin? She'd clear everything up on their way to the bakery. She wanted the job. It was an answer to so many prayers, for God to let her find a way to help her sister be happy again, happy as Leanna had been before the man she loved married someone else without telling her.

Leanna was attracted to Caleb, and he'd be a fine match for her. Outgoing where her twin was quiet. A well-respected, handsome man whose *gut* looks would be the perfect foil for her twin's. But Leanna would be too shy to let Caleb know she was interested in him. That was where Annie could help.

As she was rushing to the house, she reminded herself of one vital thing. She must be careful not to let her own attraction to Caleb grow while they worked together.

That might be the hardest part of the job.

Don't miss
The Amish Bachelor's Baby *by Jo Ann Brown,*
available February 2019 wherever
Love Inspired® books and ebooks are sold.

www.LoveInspired.com

Looking for inspiration in tales
of hope, faith and heartfelt romance?

Check out **Love Inspired**® and
Love Inspired® **Suspense** books!

New books available every month!

CONNECT WITH US AT:

Facebook.com/groups/HarlequinConnection

Facebook.com/HarlequinBooks

Twitter.com/HarlequinBooks

Instagram.com/HarlequinBooks

Pinterest.com/HarlequinBooks

ReaderService.com

LIGENRE2018R2